Let Me Be The One 2

Tina J

Copyright 2019

Caught Up Loving A Beast 1, 2 & 3

A Street King And His Shawty 1 & 2

I Fell For The Wrong Bad Boy 1&2

I Wanna Love You 1 & 2

Addicted to Loving a Boss 1, 2, & 3

I Need That Gangsta Love 1&2

Creepin With The Plug 1 & 2

All Eyes On The Crown 1,2&3

When She's Bad, I'm Badder: Jiao and Dreek, A Crazy

Love Story 1,2&3

Still Luvin A Beast 1&2

Her Man, His Savage 1 & 2

Marco & Rakia: Not Your Ordinary, Hood Kinda Love 1,2

& 3

Feenin For A Real One 1, 2 & 3

A Kingpin's Dynasty 1, 2 & 3

What Kinda Love Is This: Captivating A Boss 1, 2 & 3

Frankie & Lexi: Luvin A Young Beast 1, 2 & 3

A Dope Boys Seduction 1, 2 & 3

My Brother's Keeper 1. 2 & 3

C'Yani & Meek: A Dangerous Hood Love 1, 2 & 3

When A Savage Falls for A Good Girl 1, 2 & 3

Eva & Deray 1 & 2

Blame It On His Gangsta Luv 1 & 2

Previously...

April

After Kane left earlier, I got dressed and decided to do a little baby shopping. I had a few things here at my moms' house but the crib, stroller, and other big items I had yet to purchase.

I went into Babies'R'Us and used a scanner to put on a registry what I'd wanted. I was going to give it to Kane and let him pay for it. I walked around the store a few minutes longer and went to my car. I picked my phone up to call Kane and what do you know? He was calling me at the same time.

"Hey, I was just about to call you." I told him.

"Oh yeah. What's up?"

"Nothing. I was in the baby store ordering the crib and a few other things. I was going to see if you could put the stuff together."

"April, you and my son are coming home, and he already has everything at the house. I know it feels like forever, but baby I need you to trust me."

"I do trust you, Kane. I'm ready to come home now, but since I can't and don't know how long before I will, the baby will need something to sleep in."

"He can sleep with his mother."

"I know Kane but-"

"Stop being a brat April." I found myself pouting as I pulled up in the Cherry Hill Mall parking lot.

"Whatever."

"Do you plan on breastfeeding?" he asked me out of the blue.

"Probably not. I heard it's good for the baby, but then I heard it hurts."

"Good. Those are my titties, and I'm the only one who should be sucking on them."

"I can't with you Kane." I closed the door and headed into the mall.

"Where are you?"

"At the mall. I wanted to get me some stretch pants. I can't fit anything."

"Alright. The minute you're done I want you to go straight back to your mom's house. I don't like you being in public alone."

"You said no one knows where I am."

"I know baby, but I just want you to be careful. I'm killing everyone if anything happens to you." I smiled because he was really overprotective of me.

"Ok. I'm just running in Old Navy, and I'm leaving."

"I'm at my mom's house having dinner with everyone. You know Lexi and SJ met my brother from another mother and gave him hell. You know he said we should send your daughter to military school." I busted out laughing because she was a piece of work.

"Kane don't you let anybody send my baby away." I was laughing but dead serious.

"Hmmmm, what do I get if I don't?"

"What do you want?"

"You know what I want. Matter of fact, when you get home FaceTime me. I want to see you play with my pussy. That shit sexy as hell."

"Bye Kane. I love you."

"I love you too baby." We hung up, and I ended up staying in the mall much longer then expected.

By the time I got to my car, my feet were killing me. All I wanted to do was take a shower and lie down. Kane was probably going to come in late, and I would at least be ready for him. I loved everything about that man, and I prayed they caught the motherfucker who violated Lexi.

I brought the bags in and did exactly what I said I would. My mom left and told me she would be gone for the night. I locked up and Face Timed Kane, but he didn't answer. I assumed he was on the road to me and didn't hear the phone. I always told him to turn the music down, but he said it soothed him.

The doorbell rang while I was in the kitchen getting something to drink. I looked at the time, and it was a little after seven.

"Long time no see, baby girl," my ex, Demetrius, said and walked in without my permission. I closed my robe and even though I had on a tank top and pajama pants, I still felt naked in front of him.

"What the fuck are you doing here?" I couldn't stand my ex, and he knew it.

"Let me find out you didn't miss me."

"I didn't. What the fuck do you want?"

"I see you're expecting." I started getting nervous when he said that for some reason.

"If you don't tell me what you're here for, I'm going to call the cops." Just as I said it there was a knock at the door. He had the nerve to open it and when he did it was like the air had left my body. The nigga who violated my daughter on more than one occasion was standing in my doorway. I didn't know if I should run or call the cops. I was frozen in my spot.

"Don't be scared, April. I can guarantee he won't touch you." The nigga walked in and looked around the house as if he was trying to find something or someone."

"Demetrius, I know damn well you didn't bring this pedophile rapist in my house." I saw the surprised look on his face as if he didn't know.

11

"What are you talking about April? He's not a rapist or pedophile. You don't remember Glenn? He used to try and follow us around when we were younger." That's when it hit me.

When I dated Demetrius back then, Glenn was a few years younger and always wanted to hang with us. He was my ex's neighbor. I was standing there looking at him, and he had grown a beard, dreads, and had a mouth full of gold teeth. I would've never imagined that was him.

"Demetrius as long as we've been together when have you ever known me to lie. That nigga raped-" was all I got out when a fist connected with my face. The minute he did, I felt my mouth start bleeding and I spit out two teeth. The impact from his hit caused me to stumble, but Demetrius caught me just in time. He sat me down on the couch.

"What the fuck Glenn? Don't ever put your fucking hands on her."

I didn't know why he said that. The reason we broke up was because he was whooping my ass on a regular. I could come home from the store and run past him to use the bathroom, and that would piss him off, making him hit me a few times.

The abuse went on for the entire four years we were together. The only reason I got away from him was because he had gotten a gun charge and had to serve time. While they were arguing back and forth, I dialed Stan's number and left the phone on in my pocket.

"Call your man on the phone or I'm going to shoot your ass in the stomach. He and I have some unfinished business," Glenn said. I told him no, and he let a shot off in the ceiling.

"Her man. I see she's pregnant and all, but I thought she didn't have one."

"Nah, she goes with that nigga Kane." The look on my ex's face showed me he was about to beat my ass.

"Who the fuck is Kane?" He was in my face and spit was flying out. He yoked me up, and I prayed Stan had answered the phone and heard everything going on. I was hoping the sounds weren't muffled.

"Kane is the nigga who killed my sister?"

"Demetrius, you and I were over, and I found someone else. Please just leave." I felt myself crying. I was trying to stay calm so I wouldn't go into early labor.

He snatched me up and dragged me outside. He had me get in some car and drove off. Twenty minutes later he pulled up to some warehouse and made me go inside. I came face to face with the same bitch that lied and said she was sleeping with Stacy. There were about ten men behind her. What the hell was going on?

"What the fuck are you doing here?" She backhanded the shit out of me, and I punched her right in the nose. Her shit started leaking instantly.

"Bitch!" she yelled out, covering her nose.

"Nah, you're the bitch. Demetrius what the hell is going on and why am I here?" No one said a word as they waited for the chick to come back. She came back to me and hit me on the head with the butt of her gun. I thought Demetrius would say something, but he didn't.

"Next time I'm going to kill you," she said and sat on my ex's lap. This shit couldn't be happening right now. First, the pedophile comes to my house and hits me, then I'm dragged to a warehouse where my ex is with the chick Stacy used to be with. What the fuck else could go wrong?

"Lucy what the fuck is going on?" I turned around, and Stan, Kane, Stacy, Derrick, and a few other dudes were standing there.

"Ahhh, my loving brother and my bitch ass ex," she said sarcastically.

"How's your bitch Stacy? Too bad we didn't kill her." Stacy went to charge for her, but Stan held him back.

"April are you ok?" Kane started walking towards me but stopped when he heard a gun click. I felt it on the back of my head, and when I looked it was Glenn. I knew none of them knew it was him, but you can bet I was telling.

"How do you know my sister?" Stan asked him.

"Your sister?" Stacy and Kane said at the same time.

"Yes, we have the same father." I could see the look of confusion on Kane's face.

"Kane, we lost contact and I hadn't heard from him in years. He came back, and you and I weren't talking at first. Anyway, that's my brother, and I guess she's my sister."

"Ok, fuck this stupid ass family reunion. Stan the reason I have this dumb bitch is because I want everything you planned on passing down to her man." I saw Kane's entire face cringe.

"Are you serious right now?" Stan asked her.

"I know you're retiring, and I want the empire."

"WHAT?" he yelled out walking towards her slowly.

"How am I going to give you an empire and you barely have your memory?"

"Oh yeah, about that? I got my memory back a few years ago. I had to play dumb so I could learn everything from you. You assumed I would forget everything I heard, but I didn't."

"Lucy if you told me your memory was back, I would've groomed you for a takeover. Kane don't want the shit but the way you went about this, I'm going to have to say HELL NO to your unstable ass."

16

"It doesn't really matter because I have all your contacts and so forth. I know your bank account information and where you are hiding other money."

"If you know me like you claim to, then you would know I changed everything up, and my contacts all have new numbers and moved to new locations. My bank accounts are in another name and the ones hidden are as well." Her mouth dropped.

"You see, when you're the boss of shit, you need to make changes when no one is paying attention. That way when they think they got you by the balls, BAM! You hit them with some real shit." The look on her face was priceless.

"What the fuck Stan? I'm your sister."

"That's right, and you should've known better than to go against the grain." He shot her in the arm. I had never seen anything like it. Blood was gushing out.

Demetrius came walking towards me and put his mouth on mine. Kane fucking lost it. He was beating the shit out of him. It seemed like everything was under control until I saw

Glenn hold his phone up and there was a familiar face on the screen.

"That's right nigga. I'm the motherfucker who has your daughter."

"What?"

"That's right. She's going to be great in bed when she gets older." Kane tried to rush him, but Stacy stopped him.

"I've had someone watching your mothers' house for a week now. The minute the three of you left, I sent my boy there to get her." He showed us a photo of Lexi, and I broke down crying. I had blood coming from my mouth, and my head but the only thing concerning me was him having Lexi.

"Glenn please just let her go. You can take me," I cried out.

"Hell no April. It's me you want, right? Come on nigga. Kill me and you better hope I die because if I don't, you can bet your life I'm coming for you."

As Kane was talking, I stared a little harder at the phone he held up while his hand held the gun. There was something very familiar about the photo.

18

BOOM! was all I heard and hit the floor. I felt people stomping on me as they tried to get away.

"April, where are you?" I heard Kane yelling, but his voice was too far.

"I'm here Kane. Help me. I think I'm losing the baby." I no longer heard his voice or any other voices. My body was being lifted off the ground, and I was placed in a car. I was going in and out of consciousness.

"Kane get me to the hospital."

"My name ain't Kane bitch," was the last thing I'd heard before I passed completely out.

Kane

"HOLD THE FUCK UP." I yelled out after the gunfire stopped. I stepped over a few bodies and even moved some out of the way looking for my girl.

"Damn, I didn't even know it was these many motherfuckers in here." Stacy said. I continued looking and panicking at the same time.

"FUCKKKKKK!' I screamed out causing everybody to come to where I stood.

"April isn't here. Where the fuck is she?" As if this night couldn't get any worse.

"We have to check on Lexi." I ran out the warehouse and hopped in the car. I didn't realize Stan had the keys and he was inside making sure shit was being handled with all the dead bodies. The phone started ringing and I was praying it was my daughter or April.

"Kane I've been trying to reach you? I've been calling Stacy and he hasn't answered." Essence said when I picked up. I looked over at my brother and he was checking his pockets.

"Essence, please tell me Lexi is ok."

"Kane, uhmmm, that's what I was calling about."

"What's wrong with my daughter Essence?"

"Boy be quiet. She's fine but she wanted to talk to April. Do you know where she is because I've been calling her and no one is picking up?" I sat in the car with my head leaning back trying to decide if I should tell her over the phone or in person. Stacy must've heard her and took the phone.

"We'll be there in a few. Don't open the door for anyone; we have the key." He said a few more words to her and hung up.

"Man we have to find April. She's pregnant with my son and I'm going to lose it if anything happens to her."

"We're going to find her." I felt a little better knowing my daughter was good but then where the hell was my girl?

We got out the car and went back inside to find Stan who didn't come out the door with us. He was on the phone barking orders to someone and staring at Lucy like he wanted to murder her with his bare hands.

I stepped around him and glanced around for the

motherfucker who had my daughter on his cell phone and he was nowhere to be found. The only thing I could think of was that his ass found a way out through the shooting.

"What the fuck were you thinking Lucy?" Stan yelled in her face after he hung the phone up.

"Can we talk about that later? My arm feels like it's about to fall off."

"You think I care about that? Get your stupid ass up." He yanked her up by the arm and dragged her out the door.

"Wait!" We all stopped.

"Where is my man?"

"Your man?" Stacy asked and that made me, and Stan snap our necks and look at him. Why the fuck did he care?

"Yes. Demetrius is my man. Kane you didn't have to beat him like that."

"Man, get the fuck out of here with that." I told her and she gave me a crazy look.

"You're looking for a nigga that bounced the second he could get up."

"He wouldn't leave me." She had the nerve to seem

upset.

"Think again sis. His ass is gone. Him and that fuck nigga Glenn. But we're going to find both of them." He put her in the seat and she winced in pain. Stacy sat next to her in the back trying to comfort her. *Great*! All I need is for him to start having some sort of feelings come back for her. Essence is going to blow a fucking gasket knowing he's even this close to her.

A black van pulled up, some guys jumped out and a few minutes later the entire place was up in flames. Stan pulled out, dropped me off at the house and Stacey told me to tell Essence he would be back.

"Get out the car bro." I told him and he gave me a crazy look.

"He's right Stacy. Your fiancé is in the house and she'll be looking for you. You don't want those problems. Tell Sean I'll be back." He said and pulled off when my brother got out.

"What the fuck are you doing?" He waved me off.

"I'm serious Stacy. Essence is your soul mate, the love of your life and if you don't stay away from Lucy, you're going to throw it all away." I stopped him before we got to the door.

"Kane, I don't get in your shit with April and the late Erica so I would appreciate the same." I looked him up and down and turned my face up at him.

"You know what? You're right. But I'm going to say this, and I'll leave it alone."

"What?" He spat.

"What are you going to do when Essence finds out, leaves you and lays up with the next man?" He didn't say shit as I left him standing outside the door with a dumb look on his face. Stacy is grown and I'm not about to babysit him. If he decides to let Lucy mess up his family, then that's on him.

I opened the door and it was dark but you could see the television from the living room. Everyone was laid out on the couches and the kids were in blankets on the floor. I looked down at my daughter and almost broke down. She's been through so much in her short life and now, how am I going to explain that April is missing? That girl loved her more than Erica and everyone knew that.

I lifted her up and carried her upstairs to one of the bedrooms in my mom's house. Essence asked me where Stacy was and I pointed to the door. I laid my daughter down and watched over her in the chair on the opposite side of the room. I would've gotten in the bed with her but honestly it didn't feel appropriate for me to do that. She's been through so much that it may scare her waking up with a man lying next to her, regardless if I'm her father. If April were here it would be different.

"I thought you said Stacy was outside." Essence poked her head in the room whispering.

"He was. Maybe he ran to the house." That's the only response I could give her without explaining where he really was. This nigga is about to be on some sneaky shit with Lucy and there won't be no turning back when Essence finds out.

Me: *Yo, you don't want me in your shit and I get that but you need to contact your woman. She's looking for you.*" I hit send on my phone and put my feet up on the bed to relax. People may ask why I am here and not looking for April, but I don't know where to even start to look. If that ex nigga of hers

25

disappeared I'm sure he had her and I pray he doesn't lay a hand on her because if he does, I can't promise he'll live to see another day.

****

The next day I woke up and Lexi wasn't in the room. I stood up, stretched and went downstairs and my mom was cooking food for everyone. It was after ten and a nigga was mad as hell for sleeping that late. I should've been up looking for my girl and here it seemed like my ass didn't care.

Lexi came over and hugged me by the waist asking where April was. I couldn't tell her we had no idea so I said she stayed at her moms and she would see her soon.

"Daddy can you call her?"

"Lexi she's probably asleep. Your brother has her up all hours of the night the way he fights in her belly."

"Are you trying to say my mom doesn't want to speak to me?" She had her hand on her hips and sucked her teeth.

"What I tell you about that smart mouth shit?"

"Kane." My mom shouted out and the look she received from me made her stay out of it.

"I'm sorry. I just miss her. Can she come home today?"

"Lexi, April loves you but right now where she is, is the best place. Daddy promises she'll be home sooner than you think." She nodded her head and hugged me. I couldn't explain she's missing because I can bet, she'll assume the dude has her and think it's her fault.

"Daddy, I'll work on my attitude, but you can blame grandma and pop pop because they allow me and SJ to do and say what we want. When you come around it's hard for me to shut it off." I know damn well her ass is lying because she's scared to death to speak like that in front of April; except that one day in the hospital. I'm sure it had everything to do with my mom standing there protecting her though. That little girl will blame everyone to stay out of trouble.

"First things first Lexi. No snitching."

"Daddy, I ain't no snitch." I busted out laughing.

"What you know about snitching little girl?"

"Snitching is when a punk nigga tells everything because he don't wanna do the time." SJ said walking in with his iPad. These kids had more devices than a little.

27

"Daddy is it snitching because I told you what Glenn and Erica did?" I sat down in one of the chairs and put her on my lap.

"What did Glenn do and who is that?" SJ asked and my mom and dad looked at me.

"Remember I told you he's the one who touched me in private spots and…" SJ's entire facial expression changed.

"Why would you bring it up Lexi? You know I'm looking for him." I shook my head because SJ is a kid and overprotective as hell over his cousin. How is he looking for someone at his age? I couldn't do shit but respect his gangsta. Those two are super tight and when he asked Lexi, she put her head down.

"Don't put your head down for anyone. Do you understand me?" She nodded her head yes.

"But SJ is upset with me. Ever since he found out what happens he gets really angry and starts tearing things up." Just as she said that you heard a loud crash and we all went running in the living room. SJ stood there waiting for one of us to say something. He had a bat in his hand and the iPad he had in his hand was crushed to pieces. His face had an evil look on it and he asked if we could go look for the dude. SJ is only six but he was tall like a ten-year-old and clearly his attitude resembled his fathers and mine.

"SJ don't worry. We're going to get him." I sat down and had him do the same.

"It may seem like we're not getting him fast enough but trust me when I say everyone is out there looking for him. You have to remember too we had no idea what he looked like. Now that we do there's a reward out for his head."

"How do you know what he looks like daddy?"

"Lexi you told me." There's no way in hell I could tell her we saw him, and he got away.

"Oh yea, I forgot. SJ are you ok?"

"Yea. Don't bring his name up again Lexi." He told her and they hugged. You couldn't help but love their bond. I'm glad Erica gave my daughter up because she may have an attitude problem but seeing her and my nephews' bond is all one could ask for.

After we all ate, I told my mom the kids were staying with her and I needed to go home and change. I'm praying to hear from the nigga who has my girl.

April

"You have to push ma'am." I heard the doctor telling me. I looked around the room and Kane was standing there smiling. My man was handsome, and he was all mine.

"Baby when did you get here and how?"

"Not right now April. Just push my son out." I continued pushing and a few minutes later I heard my son screaming. Kane dropped my hand and went over to where the nurses were cleaning him up and waited. The nurse handed him the baby and he came back to me. I stared at him, stare at my son as the doctor cleaned me out.

"I should kill this bastard. This is supposed to be my motherfucking kid." I woke up to the voice of my ex. I must've been dreaming.

"What? Where am I?" I glanced around the room and I was indeed at a hospital but not sure which one. My hands instantly went to my stomach and it was still there.

"It's about time you woke the fuck up. You need to call

that fuck nigga and tell him if he ever wants to see you again, he needs to make sure Stan turns everything over to his sister." Demetrius said and handed me a phone.

"Good morning. How are you feeling?" The doctor came in smiling with a clipboard in her hand.

"How long have I been here?"

"Since last night. Your husband brought you because he thought you were in labor. Luckily you only had an accident and your water didn't break. We need to keep the baby in your stomach a little longer. Therefore, I am having you moved upstairs until you deliver."

"Oh no. I'm not staying and he's not my husband." I looked over at Demetrius and he had a dumb grin on his face. I'm sure he told them being smart.

"Oh, I'm sorry. Whoever he is, he did the right thing by getting you here. Let's get you upstairs and set up." She said. She ran over everything and had me sign some papers to be admitted.

Some guy from the transportation department came in, unhooked me from the machines and took me to a different

32

floor. After the nurse got me in the room I asked if she could stay while I took a shower. They didn't recommend it but if I peed on myself; no sponge bath was going to make me feel clean. She assisted me and I had to put that ugly ass hospital gown on. Essence needed to get her ass up here and bring me some clothes but then again, no one knows where I am. Demetrius barely spoke two words since he told me I had to call Kane.

"Call him."

'Damn is it that serious?"

"Hell yea it is. That nigga already paid and should be spreading his wealth." You could see pure greed in his eyes.

"You sound stupid as hell." I don't know why I said that. His fist connected with my face and I could've sworn I saw stars. This is the same ole nigga I tried my best to stay away from. I mean who hits a pregnant woman and has no remorse for it? He does.

I immediately started crying and split the blood out my mouth. I picked up a towel that was at the edge of my bed and covered my mouth.

"April, you know me well enough to know that talking back shit ain't going to work." He said walking to the door to close it. He pulled a gun out his back and pointed it at my stomach. I swear nothing changed about this nigga besides his age. His attitude and abuse is still very much there.

"Demetrius please."

"April, you love the nigga more than you love me?" I didn't answer and picked the phone up to dial. My answer was yes. I loved Kane more, but had it been said there's no telling what he would've done. Demetrius could snap at the drop of a dime and you never saw it coming. I couldn't risk my baby's health for it.

"You have thirty seconds to say what you need to say."

"Thirty seconds."

"Yes. You see he won't trace this call and you won't yell out where you are either because we know what will happen if you do. Now I suggest you get to it." I dialed Kane's number and prayed he didn't answer the phone.

"WHO THE FUCK IS THIS?" Kane answered the phone with so much bass in his voice.

"Kane."

"April. Baby where are you? Are you ok?" I nodded my head no forgetting he was on the phone and not in front of me.

"Twenty seconds." Demetrius said and came closer to me.

"Demetrius said Stan has to give the empire to Lucy if you ever want to see me again."

"WHAT?" I heard him blow his breath out.

"I love you April and I'm going to find you. Put that fuck nigga on the phone."

"He wants to talk to you." I handed him the phone and he put it on speaker.

"Listen here partner. You messed with the wrong woman. It's a matter of time before I find you and I can promise it won't be anything nice when I do. Your best bet is to allow my woman to leave."

"Fuck you nigga. Your woman doesn't seem like she's hurting to me. The two of us are laid up like we used to be. I can say her body is still soft and that pussy is about to be touched."

"Yo! I swear if you." You could hear the anger in Kane's voice when Demetrius spoke about touching me.

"Nah, I'm in charge nigga. If you want her back in one piece do what the fuck I said." Demetrius hung up before Kane could respond. I looked at him as the idiot he was. How is he going to tell me make sure we hung up in thirty seconds and he was on the phone longer?

"Damn, that nigga in love huh? What you do to him?" He asked and licked his lips. I rolled my eyes and turned over to take a nap. He was irking the hell out of me.

I felt him rubbing on me and smacked his hand away. Demetrius had a way of making my skin crawl. It most likely came from him hitting and cheating on me. Once a woman gets fed up, she can't stand to be around or touched by the man.

"You go ahead and take a nap. I'll be back but April." He stopped before he got to the door.

"What?"

"If you put your hands on me again, I'll knock the shit out of you." He walked out the door laughing. *God please let*

36

Kane find me. I said a prayer before I went to sleep. After an hour of him not returning, I called the nurse and asked if I could use her cell phone.

"April, tell me this is you." Kane spoke in the phone.

"Kane come get me please."

"Where are you?" I could hear keys in the background and told him I had no idea.

He told me to put someone on the phone who could tell him. He spoke to the nurse and next thing I know she said he was on the way. I tried to wait for him to get there but ended up falling asleep.

****

I'm not sure how long I was asleep but when I woke up, my man was lying in the bed next to me. I had to pinch myself to make sure it wasn't another dream. He stared down at me and tears formed in my eyes. Wondering when he got here didn't matter. The fact he was lying next to me was enough.

"Baby did that nigga touch you?" He asked rubbing his hand down the side of my face and placed a soft kiss on my lips.

"He tried, but I smacked his hand away. Kane did you find him?"

"Right now all that matters is you're ok and so is my son. They said you had to stay but it's not happening."

"Kane the doctor said…"

"I don't care. You're coming home and my mom…"

"Hell no. Your mom nothing." He started laughing.

"April stop acting like that."

"No Kane. She and I will deal with one another on the strength of the baby but that's it. You can say what you want but she still believes it's my fault Glenn got to Lexi." I stopped talking and remembered the night all the shit happened, and Lexi came to mind.

"Oh my God. Where is my daughter?" I removed the blanket from my legs, and he stopped me.

"April calm your ass down. Lexi is fine and she's at the house waiting for you. As far as my mom, if you don't want her around I'll respect it. I can't take away how you feel about the situation. All I ask, is the two of you are cordial when you're around one another." He can say what he wants but his mom blames me and I'll never forget how she treated me over it. Lexi is a child so me holding it against her would be childish, but his mom fucking knows better.

The doctor came in with discharge papers and explained to me it wasn't a good idea to leave but she couldn't force me to stay either. She told us everything that needed to be done and since Kane paid for a nurse to come by daily, she handed me some forms for her too. Kane gave me some leggings and a shirt to throw on. He said he wouldn't walk out with me in a gown. The nurse wheeled me downstairs and he ran to get the car. I couldn't wait to get home.

****

"Hey mommy." Lexi ran to me when I walked in the house. Essence and Sean came to give me a hug but the look on Stan's face made me nervous.

"What's wrong?" I asked him.

"Sis, I know you just got out the hospital, but we need every bit of information you have on him. Not only does your ex want the empire but he's been working with the feds to take me down." I covered my mouth.

"But how?"

"Sis, when he was in jail, he somehow met Lucy through a mutual friend. Lucy thought he loved her and began to tell him all the information she had on me and agreed to try and do a takeover. However, we were able to stop it but now Lucy is missing again and there's no telling where they are or what's going on." I nodded my head and gave them all the information I had on him. Hopefully, the information would be good enough because I rid my life of him years ago.

Everyone stayed at the house for a few hours, and after they left, I told Kane my body was tired. He locked the door and told Lexi to go bathe. SJ was staying over too so he made him do the same.

I moved the covers back and went to lie down but he stopped me and had me go in the bathroom. They told me not to walk too much and if Kane could've carried me, he would've. The bath water he set for me was warm and Lord knows my ass didn't need to take one, but it was calling me. I stayed in there for at least twenty minutes when Kane told me he had to check on the kids. He wanted to make sure they took showers and got ready for bed.

"How are you and my son doing?" He asked, lifted me up and sat behind me. His hands rubbed my stomach as he kissed on my neck.

"We're good baby. I missed you."

"I missed you too baby." His hands massaged my chest and found their way to my pearl, which he caressed under the water.

"April, I'm sorry that nigga got to you."

"It's ok baby. I knew you would find me. Oh shittttt." I moaned out and released myself.

"I needed that." I leaned my head back and kissed him.

"Help me up Kane."

"Why? You don't want to take a bath with me." He stood and helped me but washed us up first.

"Go slow baby." He held on to me tight; making sure I didn't fall. Kane may be an ignorant motherfucker in the streets but with me he's gentle as hell. He dried me off and instead of throwing clothes on, I let my towel drop and he smiled staring at my stomach. Kane was excited to have a child

41

with me and the feeling is definitely mutual.

"Mmmmm April. You're sucking the hell out of my dick." He grabbed my hair and pumped slowly in and out. Slob leaked out my mouth making it sloppy as hell the way he enjoyed it.

"Cum for me Kane. Let me know you missed me."

"Awww shit April. Fuckkkkk." He came instantly and I swallowed every drop.

"Baby we can't have sex for a while. I hope me doing that will be enough for you not to stray. I swear I'll have lock jaw if you need me to do it every night."

"April. You are all I need and want in a woman. I would never risk what we have for some random pussy. I'm aware of what the doctor said and you and my son's health mean everything to me. If your man has to wait, then it is what it is but baby don't think it will make me cheat because it won't."

"I know but…"

"Yea, when you left a while ago, I almost slipped up with Sherri, but I didn't think you were coming back to me."

He made me look at him.

"April when that shit happened in the hospital and we didn't speak or see one another there wasn't a woman out there who could take your spot. You were the only woman on my mind, and it will stay that way. You're going to be my wife and have all my kids. No woman on this earth is worth losing you. I love you and what we have too much for that to happen." I cried and he sat me down on his lap.

"My son has you being a crybaby. I need the evil April who gave me a lap dance at the club." I laughed and wiped my eyes.

"I got you baby when your son comes." He smiled.

"Damn, how did a nigga get this lucky?" He pecked my lips and had me lay back on the bed. I assumed he was getting in the bed with me but instead he gave me a full body massage and put his mouth on the place he loved the most and my body succumbed to him more than once. He asked how he got so lucky but to be honest, I feel like the lucky one.

Demetrius

"Yo, Glenn where you at?" I yelled in my house. After the shootout in the warehouse he snatched April up and waited for me in the car. It was so much going on that no one knew we were out until it was too late.

At first Glenn wanted to kill my ex but that shit ain't happening. We may not be together, but she is still the only woman I ever loved.

April and I were good together, but I can admit my hands were a problem during our relationship.

In the beginning it was the two of us against the world and no one could tell us shit. However, my ass started cheating and anytime I came home she would accuse me. My anger would escalate and cause me to put hands on her. The first time it happened I couldn't believe it. Then it continued happening and since she didn't leave, it became more and more common. Mind control is a crazy thing. It can have a person like your robot and that's what April used to be to me. It may be fucked up, but it is what it is.

When I first got released from jail, Glenn picked me up and I told him April was a priority in my life and I needed to find her. Imagine my surprise when he told me where she was. The day I stopped by her moms' house and she opened the door pregnant I was hurt. She was supposed to wait for me and have my children. I guess being locked up she regained her self-esteem. In a way it was good, but for me it was a bad thing.

After she called Glenn a pedophile rapist and he hit her, I was pissed and curious. Glenn used to be around us all the time and not once has anyone ever accused him of something so major. Yea, he may have stuck a few kids up here or there and sold drugs but nothing like what she accused him of.

A pedophile and rapist are serious and if that's true his ass will be dealt with. He thinks he has to worry about those niggas but if it's true I'm taking his life. The nigga Kane and me may not know each other but doing that to a child is something I can't accept.

"Yo, I just got out the shower." He came in the living room in a towel and I heard a woman laughing.

"My bad. I didn't know you had company." The woman stood behind him in a towel licking her lips. What the hell is wrong with women? She's here with him and lusting over me. I told him we would speak later and went to my room. I came out the shower and laid in my bed in just a towel smoking a blunt.

"Yo. I'll be back." Glen yelled out as he opened my door.

"Alright. Bring me back some wraps." I handed him the money, but he declined and said he had it. I dosed off and woke up to someone sucking my dick. I wanted it to be April, but she was in the hospital, so I assumed it was Jackie.

"Suck that shit." I looked down and had no idea who the chick was but couldn't say anything because my nut was at the tip.

"Damn girl. That shit was the bomb. Who are you?" Home girl sat on top of me kissing down my neck and waking my man back up.

"Do you have a condom?" She asked and I pointed to the nightstand.

"Damn your dick is big as hell." She slid down and squeezed her pussy muscles together. Shorty has some good pussy and the two of us went at it for almost an hour. I still didn't ask how she got in and she didn't answer when I asked who she was.

Once I came in the condom shorty put a towel on and that's when I remembered who she was. This is the same chick who had just showered with Glenn. *What the fuck?*

"Are you crazy? How you in here on my dick when you fucking Glenn?" She laughed.

"Glenn and I are fuck buddies. We damn sure screw who we want so don't worry about it."

"Oh word. Y'all fuck roommates too." I questioned her and she came closer to me.

"No, but when you came in my pussy got wet and that never happens. Something about you is dangerous and it's the type of man I like." She ran her hand up and down my pole.

"You didn't like it."

"I didn't say that. I'm saying this won't happen again."

"I think it will." This chick got on her knees and

pleased me again. I can't front her dick sucking skills are nice and we indeed will continue this at a later date. If they're not in a relationship who am I to deprive her of this good dick.

"Yo, put your number in my phone." She smirked and did it. I looked down at my phone to see who she saved it under, so I know who to call.

"Sherri. I'll see you." She waved and walked out.

****

That shit put me straight to sleep and I didn't wake up until the next day. I got dressed and headed over to the hospital. I probably should've stayed there all night but April is on bed rest and admitted. She isn't going anywhere and I'm sure she wouldn't call her man because I threatened her.

I stepped off the elevator and went to her room only to be told she checked out an hour ago. I guess she didn't take my warning to heart. Now I have to show and prove to show her I'm not playing.

"Hey Demetrius. What are you doing here?" Her mom asked when she opened the door.

"Not much. I just came home and decided to stop by

and visit you." She and I had a great relationship that's why me shooting her in the chest hurt me more than it did her.

"If you survive, tell your daughter this is just the beginning."

I walked out the house and shut the door. My cell was ringing, and it was Jackie telling me she was at some hotel and to come visit her. I'm not sure if it's a trick or not so I had her give me the address and said I'd be there later. I picked the phone up and dialed 911 to report a shooting at April's mom house. You see I shot her, but she is the only one who could tell my ex who did it. Her man will come for me and I will be standing there waiting.

Stacy

Seeing Lucy over the last year in her stalking phase was enough to make me want to kill her. But after laying eyes on her the other night at the warehouse had me looking at her different. She has always been a gorgeous woman, but she held this sort of boss bitch power trying to take over Stan's empire. I'm not going to lie and say it didn't turn me on because it did. What I didn't or couldn't understand is why my feelings were starting to resurface after all this time? My woman is definitely my soul mate like Kane said but Lucy being in my presence did something to me.

"Stacy you do know Essence won't be happy if she finds out." Lucy said standing over me in a bra and panties. Her body is still bad as hell and would make any man strip to jump in bed with her.

"Who said she's going to find out?" I stood up and moved her out the way. She came closer and kissed me. Instead of pushing her off I fucked up and parted her lips with my tongue. She wrapped her legs around me and for the moment it felt good, but I couldn't do that to Essence and forced her off me.

"What the hell Stacy?" She asked mad as hell.

"I have a girl."

I know everyone is thinking we slept together but that is far from the truth. Lucy may be gorgeous, and my dick may be hard right now staring at her body but it's not enough to make me cheat on Essence.

I thought about what my brother said to me on the porch and took my ass home to take a cold shower. All pussy is different and that's no secret but what my woman has is not anything I'm willing to share. If she ever found out I cheated on her and went to another man, my son wouldn't have a mother. No other man will ever feel in between her legs and that's real nigga shit.

"You mean to tell me she isn't worried about where you are? It's midnight and you're here with me."

"What?" I hopped off the couch and looked for my keys that were in my pocket when I got there and now they weren't.

I had Lucy in a hotel to keep her away from Stan. I had been keeping her company until she could get away from him. Granted she could've took a flight out but after she disappeared at the hospital, he didn't take any chances on that happening and had people looking for her there. Anyway, she asked me to come watch a movie with her and that was fine but a nigga fell asleep. I should've never helped her ass out.

"Don't worry. I let her know on the phone where you were." I turned around to say something and there was a knock on the door.

"Open it." She smiled and as bad as I wanted to jump out the window, I had to face the consequences of my actions.

"You're out looking for Lucy with Stan, huh?" Essence said pushing me to the side and walking in the room. That's where I told her I would be when I left the house and here I was busted in a lie.

"Essence let me explain."

"No need. Lucy here told me everything."

"I'm not sure what she told you, but what it is, is a lie."

"Oh the kiss we shared is a lie?" Essence looked like

52

the devil when Lucy shouted that out.

"Oh you two chilling with one another and kissing. What's next Stacy, sex?"

"Essence she kissed me."

"And you kissed me back. It was tongue too." Lucy said rubbing it in and smirking.

"I came to see if it were true. I'm gone." Essence said limping out and that was the worst thing I could've let Lucy see.

"Stacy how are you fucking her crippled ass? No wonder you're over here with me. Her ass can barely walk which means she ain't riding that dick or fucking you right."

"Yo, don't ever talk about her like that. You did that shit to her." I pushed her in to the wall.

"You're the one who had me shot?" She walked over to Lucy. I had to hold her back because Essence was no joke with the hands.

"Damn right. I'd do it again if I had a gun on me now." Essence tried getting out of my grasp.

"Put me down Stacy." She hollered out while we were

by the elevators. I snatched her up out the room to avoid a fight.

"Calm down baby." She smacked me across the face so hard my face turned.

I couldn't even say anything because I deserved it. She stepped on the elevator and I tried to get on with her and she told me no and to go back with my ex. I could see her tears falling and wanted to wipe them, but the doors closed.

I felt my pockets for my keys and realized they were still in the room. Lucy never closed the door and had a sneaky ass grin on her face. Kane was right. I should've left her dumb ass in the past and now look.

"Where are my keys?" Lucy backed up and slid them in her panties. I was over playing these damn games with her.

"Give me my keys yo." She sat back with her legs open and I could see her shaved pussy in those see through panties. My dick didn't get hard this time because my focus stayed on Essence and getting to her. I snatched her up and stuck my hand down there to get them. I went in the bathroom to wash my hands and rinse off my keys without messing up the alarm.

I hopped in my car and thought about calling Kane, but

I could hear him now saying I told you so. Plus, his girl came home from the hospital and he wasn't really trying to leave her.

My house was a block away and I could see shit being tossed out the windows when I drove down the street. How in the hell did she get here so fast? I jumped out the car and ran over to pick some of it up. We didn't need these neighbors in our business.

"GET THE FUCK OUT STACY. GO BACK TO YOUR EX WHO CAN FUCK YOU BETTER THAN ME." I could hear the pain in her voice as she said it.

"Essence I'm sorry." I tried pleading with her but she didn't wanna listen.

"You're just like the rest of these niggas who apologize only because he got caught; but guess what, you can spend all the time in the world with her now."

"I don't want her Essence. I was helping her out to keep Stan from killing her." She chuckled and threw her head back.

"I don't care what she did to make her brother want to kill her but if it's the truth she had to do something that warranted it. What I'm trying to figure out is why you feel the

55

need to help her? She's the ex who stalked you for what a year and you never told me"

"Stacy, the kiss is not excusable at all, and we may have been able to move past it but what I can't get over is how you protected a woman who almost killed me. STACY, I CAN BARELY FUCKING WALK AND ALMOST LOST MY LIFE AND CHANCE AT HAVING KIDS AGAIN AND YET, YOU'RE SITTING IN A FUCKING HOTEL ROOM WITH HER CHILLING." She screamed out.

"Essence I swear I'm sorry. I wasn't thinking." I couldn't take seeing my woman like this and it was killing me inside. She and I had arguments before, and we got over them. This one right here though was different and at any time she's about to say its over and I can't have that.

"Sorry huh? You damn right you're sorry. A sorry excuse for a man. You're supposed to protect your family, not protect the one who almost destroyed it."

"Essence." She sat down on the steps crying.

"Just go Stacy."

"No. I'm sorry and we can get through this."

"We can get through a lot Stacy, but this is the ultimate disrespect and I can't do it anymore. You were scared to tell me she stalked you, yet, you left me in the dark and she could've attacked me at anytime and I wouldn't have known why. Then, she almost kills me and when you find her, you comfort her. What am I missing? What type of man doesn't get rid of the person who tried to kill his future wife? Do you still love her? I mean that's the only reason I could think of as to why you're protecting her."

"Honestly, Essence there's no love left in me for her. Seeing her again made my feelings come back but not enough to ever wanna be with her in that way. I'm not sure why I protected her. Yes, we were together a long time ago but that's it. Maybe I protected her because if Stan killed her, he would regret it later and I didn't want that."

"That's not your concern Stacy. I am, well I was. I should've been put first instead of lied to or cheated on." I gave her a look.

"A kiss is still cheating Stacy. How could you? You know what? This conversation is over. I don't wanna be with you." She couldn't finish her sentence before I had her yoked up by the throat on those steps.

"We are never going to be over Essence. Do you fucking hear me?" She nodded her head yes with tears falling down her face.

"I messed up baby, but I swear you are the only woman I want." I let her down and she started swinging. Her punches made it to my face; my side and she kicked me so hard in my stomach I had to catch myself from falling. I've never put my hands on her like this but her ending us had me losing it.

"Essence please talk to me." I begged her through the door that she ran in and locked.

I sat there with my back to the door for a long time and refused to leave without her saying we were still getting married. People can say what they want but what they don't realize is men cry behind closed doors. When you love a person as much as I love her and she ends it, it's not an easy pill to swallow. I've never once cheated or put my hands on her in all the time we've been together, so I know she was hurting.

"Let's go bro." I looked up and both Kane and Stan were standing there looking at me shaking their heads.

"I'm not leaving so y'all may as well go." I stood up, walked in our room and laid down on the bed. I felt the bed sink in on two sides.

"Look man. You fucked up and not only cheated but you put your hands on her. What we're you thinking? And why the fuck is Lucy with you when you know I've been looking for her?" Kane sat there not saying anything while Stan questioned me.

"She's not leaving me." I said ignoring the question about his sister.

"Stacy get the fuck up and leave." Kane said and stood up.

"What?"

"You heard what the fuck I said. You did this shit nigga. I fucking told your ass not to mess with Lucy, but you told me to stay out of it and I did. You snuck off with her and even though you said nothing happened but a kiss, you had no business with her when you had a good woman at home. You think you can boss Essence around into being with you and that shit ain't right. Man the fuck up and go." Kane said with bass in his voice.

"Fuck you Kane. You think you're better than me, but you aren't. You're going to mess up and cheat on her too. Then what?" I tried to make him feel like shit. Him throwing *I told you so* in my face pissed me off.

"Hold up Stacy." Stan said and stood in the middle of us.

"How you going to get mad at him for telling you how it is? You did this, not him. Had you stayed away this wouldn't be happening. You're mad at the wrong person."

"Nah. This nigga couldn't wait to rub it in my face."

"Is that what you think nigga." I could tell Kane was getting pissed.

"You think I wanted to hear your girl crying on the phone to April saying you put your hands on her and you cheated. You think I wanna deal with someone else's bullshit when I'm trying to keep my family safe and find a nigga WHO RAPED MY FUCKING DAUGHTER? YOU REALLY

THINK I WANNA BE HERE. I'M LEAVING MY FAMILY
UNPROTECTED TO DEAL WITH SOMETHING I TOLD
YOU NOT TO DO. FUCK YOU NIGGA." I saw Essence
come out the bathroom. Her and Stan were both giving me a
fucked up look.

"Man, my bad." I felt like shit when he mentioned the
shit with my niece. He was right about this being my fuck up.

"Nah nigga. Don't feel bad now. You damn sure didn't
feel bad when you said it so don't take it back."

"Kane, I'm sorry for calling April." Essence said and
he hugged her.

"Don't be sorry Essence. She's your best friend and
you needed her. I figured it's only right to come get him but it
looks like he doesn't give a fuck about anyone but himself.
Fuck everyone, is how he feels and you know what? That's the
mentality I have to be on too. I can't give a fuck about anyone
but my family now."

"Kane man I'm sorry." I grabbed his arm as he went to
step out.

"Get the fuck off me Stacy."

"Calm the fuck down Kane." I told him and he punched me in the face. The two of us started squaring up and Essence was yelling in the background. We heard a gun go off and stopped.

"Cut this shit out. You two are brothers." My pops came in going off. My dad stayed in the background of a lot of things, but I guess Essence called my mom and sent him.

"I'm good pops. I need to get to my family." Kane said and tried to leave. He reached down in his pocket and grabbed his phone.

"Kane stay your ass right there." He stopped and turned around while he was on the phone.

"Pops, I love you but right now April needs me."

"See there he goes running to her again. We need to deal with this shit." I told him.

"FUCK YOU NIGGA." He came over to me.

"You damn right I'm running to her. My fucking girl's mother was shot and they don't know if she's going to make it but hey, let's all stay here and make sure Stacy is ok."

"What?" Essence yelled out.

"Man, I don't have time for this shit. I'm gone and Stacy you need to stay away from me and my family since their such a fucking inconvenience." He ran out the house and I heard his car speed off.

Stan, my pops and Essence gave me the look of death. I can't believe I allowed Lucy in my life again and caused so much pain, I lost my girl and my brother. *What the fuck was I thinking?*

April

"Is she going to be ok?" I asked the nurse about my mom when we got to the hospital. We weren't able to leave when the call came in because we had to drop Lexi and SJ off at his moms' house. I'm not sure what happened when he went over to his brothers' house, but he came back pissed off. I didn't want to say anything, and he take it out on me, but he'll tell me eventually.

"I'm not sure what's going on ma'am. I just came on shift but give me a few minutes to find out some information for you." She said and Kane made me sit down next to him.

"She's going to be fine baby." Kane lifted my hand and kissed the back of it and I put my head on his shoulder.

"I hope so. Who would do this to her? Do you think it's one of those home invasions?" He shrugged his shoulders and leaned his head back.

"Kane are you ok?"

"I'm good. I'm just worried about you."

"And I'm worried about you. What happened?" He ran

his hand down his face and explained to me everything that happened. I couldn't believe Stacy did that to Essence. She told me bits and pieces because Kane jumped out of bed to go over there. Then to find out they argued and had a fight made shit worse. I squeezed his hand and told him everything happens for a reason, but it will all work itself out. I'm not sure why Stacy threw me in there, but it's pretty fucked up that he blamed everyone but himself.

"Hi Ms. Brown." The nurse said coming our direction.

"Your mom is still in surgery but the doctor wanted to inform you, he will speak to you as soon as he done." I thanked the nurse and went back to speaking with Kane.

"You can go Kane." I told him and leaned back in my seat.

"Nah. I'm good." He grabbed my face and kissed my lips.

I stared at Kane and as much as I didn't want to say what's about to leave my mouth it had to be done. I loved my man, Lexi and my son probably more than I loved myself but the shit between his mom and I, and now his brother, is too much.

Dealing with my ex, we didn't have this issue because he was the only child. And even with everything going on he's trying to destroy what Kane and I have too. I looked over to say something and his eyes were closed. *So much for the talk.* I guess it will happen later.

The doctor came out an hour later and told us the surgery went well and that I could see her.

When we stepped in, the doctor she had been dealing with sat there kissing her hand. I was happy to see my mom experiencing love again after my father. A lot of people think after a certain age you can't fall in love but my mom proves that to be a myth everyday.

Stan came in with Sean and Essence and he started crying. Stan is like my mom's son too so I knew he would take seeing her like this just as hard.

"The bullet went through the right side of her chest. Luckily it missed major organs. I don't know what I would do if I lost her." The guy said. I'm not sure why he relayed the same information the other doctor did but fuck it.

"Did they say when she'll wake up?" He wiped his eyes and stood up.

"Yea. She should wake up after the anesthesia wears off. Listen, I have to run home and get dressed."

"You have to work."

"Yes but I'm taking off. What do I look like having my woman in here and I'm not by her side?" He smiled and kissed me on the cheek. He shook Stan and Kane's hand and then asked about Lexi before he left. It wasn't anything we could do but wait it out.

Kane sat me on his lap and rubbed my belly. When he did that my son would always kick. He knew his father's touch out of everyone else who rubbed it. We sat there for hours waiting for my mom to wake up.

"I love you Kane." He lifted my legs on his lap and kissed me. It's gonna be a long night.

****

"Hi everyone." We looked up and my mom was awake smiling. I glanced at my phone and it was after eight in the morning. We had been here all night. I jumped off Kane's lap and he yelled and told me to calm down before my son came too early.

"Mommy. Are you ok? Do you know who did this?"

"April I'm fine. You're always worried about everyone else. Now calm down like Kane said before you go into early labor."

"Mom who did this?" At first, she didn't wanna answer. Stan had to make her tell us by saying he wouldn't come back to see her if she didn't. He had been away for so long she didn't want to risk him disappearing again.

"Demetrius."

"Excuse me." I asked making sure she said the right name.

"It was your ex." I glanced over at Kane and Stan and the two of them were walking out making phone calls.

"Are you sure? Why would he do this to you?"

"Honey that man still loves you." I put my head down.

"I'm with Kane and..."

"Honey, I didn't tell you that for you to be with him. I told you because a man in love will do dangerous things to get a woman's attention. This isn't the right way to go about it but he knew you'd come running. He made sure not to kill me so I could tell who did it."

"But why?"

"I don't know April and it's not up for you to figure it out. That man out there loves you to death. Don't go trying to solve shit on your own. Let him and your brother handle it."

"I'm not going to let him come shoot you and think everything is ok."

"April listen to your mom." Essence spoke up.

"Demetrius is crazy and we all know it. If you go sticking your nose in shit; not only are you going to mess up what you and Kane have but put your own self in danger." I listened to her and my mom speak and noticed Sean not saying anything.

"Are you ok?" I asked her and she nodded.

"I think you should listen April." Sean spoke and came to where I sat.

"They're going to kill him and you need to make sure you're far away when it happens." I covered my mouth. Not because Demetrius didn't deserve it but knowing he's going to die because of me had me thinking too hard on the situation.

Stan and I stayed with my mom all day talking, laughing and reminiscing about the old days. Kane left and brought me some clothes to change in. Lexi didn't allow him to leave without bringing her to see me today. She had everyone hysterical the entire time.

It started to get late and Kane called his mom and asked if she could pick Lexi up. He went down stairs when she came and called up ten minutes later and said to send Stan down with her, but I needed to get out the room, so I took her. Why didn't I listen and let him take her down? When I got to where they were Lexi had run in front of me but neither Kane nor his mom turned around. They must've assumed Stan brought her and left.

"Kane she's causing too many problems with this family. She isn't speaking to me and how dare you leave your brother who is going through something to run to her? You need to leave her"" Kane ran his hand down his face.

"April doesn't speak to you because of what you blame

70

her for."

"I still do."

"Exactly. Why would she want to associate herself with you? As far as Stacy, he is a grown ass man. I told him to leave Lucy alone."

"I don't care what you say; April has to go. You're going to end up back in jail." She said and took Lexi's hand in hers. Thank goodness she had earphones in. I backed up and made my way to the elevators. His mother was right. We needed to leave each other alone and that's exactly what I'm going to do.

"You good?" Kane questioned me after coming to the room twenty minutes later.

"Yup. I'm perfect." Stan and Kane looked at each other. I shouldn't be mad at him but that's his mother and even though he said something to her I can't be with someone whose family feels like that. It will be a constant battle between us and I loved Kane too much to put him through that.

****

I stayed at the hospital for the next week with my mom.

71

Essence came to pick me up today because the two of us were going to my moms' house to clean up. I told her to come stay with us, but she said Stacy wasn't running her out the house.

We pulled up and there were two detectives out there. Of course, when we got out they asked a million questions but I didn't say anything. They left their card and without so much as a goodbye. They know we knew who did it but wouldn't tell. Cops hate the no snitching rule and right now so did I. How could I not tell who shot her? My mom made me promise to allow Kane and Stan to handle it but I wanted him to go to jail right now; not when he came out of hiding.

"What's up with you April?" Essence asked turning off the vacuum.

"Nothing." Essence knew me better than anyone so me telling her that wasn't a good answer. She patted the seat next to her on the couch for me to join her.

"Essence, Kane's mother hates me and I'm tired of her kicking my back in."

"What are you talking about?"

I was about to answer her, but Kane and Stan came by.

I wiped my eyes in hopes they wouldn't see. Both of them were always concerned about the baby and me. If either of them saw me crying it would be like an interrogation until they knew what was wrong.

"Hey baby." He kissed my lips.

He and I hadn't been speaking since the day his mom was talking shit. I should tell him but at the same time he should tell me how his mom feels too. He helped me get up and followed me to the kitchen. Stan stayed in the living room talking to Essence when in walked Stacy and I knew then shit was about to hit the fan.

Kane

The day my mom picked Lexi up from the hospital April has been acting very standoffish and I'm not sure why. I came back to the room and her entire attitude towards me was different.

Over the last two weeks she stayed at the hospital while I went home tending to Lexi and trying to find those two niggas. They had to be hiding out or left town because we hadn't heard anything from them. It's all-good though because Stan had his people working on it so it will be a matter of time before we find them.

Today Stan and I were going to help April and Essence clean her moms' house. She was due to come home from the hospital in a few days. Her man asked her to stay with him and she said yes but that she needed her place cleaned up too. I don't know how much April thought she was doing being she is supposed to be on bed rest. I've witnessed her a few times making facial expressions because she was in pain. At the time, she was in a hospital so if anything happened, we didn't have

74

to worry. I planned on talking to her ass about what the hell she had going on in her mind.

I helped her off the couch and went in the kitchen with her. Unfortunately, my brother walked in and it seemed like everyone stopped speaking.

"Why are you here?" Essence asked and he sucked his teeth. Neither of us have spoken to one another since the night we fought. I had nothing to say to him and I'm sure the feeling's mutual. Who asks their brother to pick him over his girl for some shit that could've been avoided?

"Essence we need to talk."

"Not right now Stacy. I'm helping my best friend."

"And." I felt my fist balling up.

"Kane please." April whispered. I had to keep calm, or I was about to flip the hell out on him.

"Look nigga. I get this break up is hurting but you're going to stop coming for my fiancé. She didn't do shit to you."

"I'm over the shit with your bitch." He couldn't say anything else because I had knocked his ass out. Well not hard enough for him to hit the ground but enough to shut the fuck up.

"Oh my God Kane." I heard April screaming. He got up and wiped his lip but didn't even try to hit me back because he knew his ass was wrong.

"Stacy, why do you keep talking shit about April? She didn't do anything to you and that's your brothers' fiancé. He has never spoken to me like that and I think you need to respect her like he does me." Essence tried to get him to see it her way, but he wasn't listening.

"You want to know why I don't fuck with her." We all stood there listening.

"If Kane never fucked with her, her dumb ass ex wouldn't have come back with mine and we'd still be together." We all looked at him like he was crazy.

"Stacy you did that to yourself. It didn't matter if he came back or not, that bitch, excuse me Stan." She turned around to say but he waved her off like he didn't care what she said about Lucy.

"April didn't make you rent a room for her, spend time with her, kiss her or even allow her to live after you know she's the one who did this to me. YOU DID THAT SHIT ALL ON YOUR OWN STACY. TAKE RESPONSIBILITY FOR WHAT YOU DID AND STOP BLAMING EVERYONE ELSE." Essence was mad as hell.

"Let's go Essence."

"No. Why do you want to be with this crippled bitch? Ain't that what Lucy said?" When she said that all of us looked at him. April had tears coming down her face.

"WHAT?" Stan yelled out.

"Oh yea you didn't know. Lucy told me I'm too crippled for Stacy and that's why he dipped out. How could I ride his dick or fuck you right? That's what she said isn't it Stacy? I mean you may as well tell them why she had you spending all your free time there."

"You know what Essence? Fuck you. You don't want to be with me anymore then I'm out."

"Bye." She said with no concern at all. Stacy turned around and stared at her.

"I never slept with her Essence. I wouldn't do that to you. Yes, the kiss was fucked up but as far as you not sexing me right because of what happened has never been a problem. I see now that maybe I should go ahead and sleep with her and everyone else since you being crippled or whatever you call yourself, won't fuck with me." He spoke in a calm voice to her.

"I knew you looked at me like that." He ran up on her.

"Never Essence. I proposed to you after the accident, but the ring has been waiting for years to go on your finger. I was just too scared to ask." He looked down at her hand.

"You don't want me anymore. Then you don't need this ring." He slid that shit off her finger and left. If you ask me, she should've been taken it off if she wasn't marrying him. That told me she was acting off emotions and most likely would have taken him back.

"Ummm, Kane we need to talk." April said and asked me to follow her upstairs. Stan stayed with Essence who was now hysterical crying.

I closed the door to the room and lifted April's shirt over her head. I knew she was mad and had to get her to relax before she spoke. She stepped outta her pants and moved back on the bed. I slid her panties down and went in for the kill. She grabbed my head and squeezed my neck while releasing her juices in my mouth.

"You good now." She sat up and moved me in front of her as she sat on the bed.

"I'm good, but now its time to make sure you are." She winked and pulled my man out. My girl gave the best head and anytime she did I would be fine not having sex. I guess since she's been on bed rest It was something I had to deal with and got used to it.

"Just like that April. Shit baby." I shot my babies down her throat and the two of us got in the shower. I wanted badly to make love to her, but we were both scared about the baby coming soon. She would be eight months tomorrow, but we still didn't wanna take any chances. I helped her dry off and put on her long pajama shirt. Between this house and ours she had stuff to wear and kept things here for me too. That's why she's about to be my wife. No one can top her, and I'll be damned if anyone tries to.

"Kane." I turned over and stared at her.

"I think we should take a break." I rolled on my back to keep myself calm.

"April. What are you talking about?" I stared at the ceiling listening to her speak that bullshit.

"I'm just saying, your mom and I aren't speaking, and your brother blames me for the two of you not speaking and what him and Essence went through."

"Who the fuck cares April?" I didn't mean to be blunt with it but she was pissing me off.

"I care Kane. That's your family and I don't want to cause friction between y'all."

"April, right now you aren't making any sense. Say what you mean." There was something on her mind she's holding back.

"Fine Kane. The day at the hospital, I heard your mom blaming me for what happened to Lexi. She doesn't like me and I'm not about to kiss her ass to make her either." I sat up in the bed.

"Did I ask you to kiss anyone's ass? Huh? Did I ever tell you, you had to speak to her? As far as Stacy that's his shit he's going through."

"Kane. It's just…"

"Its' just what April." I started putting my clothes on.

"You don't understand what it feels like being around people who don't like you."

"That's because I don't give a fuck if people like me April. I am who I am and I'm going to be with who I want regardless if my mother approves."

"I'm telling you how I feel and you're yelling."

"Damn right I'm yelling. You are about to be my wife and now you wanna tell me you want to take a break over some bullshit. If you want the nigga who came back for you then go ahead April. I'm not into fighting over no bitches." I could tell in her face she was hurt. She stood up and walked over to where I sat putting my shoes on.

"I don't want that motherfucker Kane and you of all people should know that."

"Why should I know April? Because you're pregnant by me and accepted my proposal? It don't mean shit when the woman you love is breaking up with you. I told you before fuck what my mom thought and you were ok with it. Now all of a sudden this nigga pops up and you're changing but I get it."

"Kane stop saying that. I don't want him." She started crying and I gave zero fucks. She fucked me up and I was hurting so she should too.

"I'm not so sure April. This break will be what you need to figure that out, but I can tell you that I'm not sitting around waiting for you to get your emotions in check. I know you're pregnant and hormonal, but you still know what the fuck you're saying."

"I want to be happy Kane."

"And I don't. April you and my daughter make me happy. I'm not worried about anyone or anything but the two of you and now my son, but you can't see that. You're being selfish as fuck right now and honestly I'm over fighting my family for you."

"I know you are."

"April, I will go to fucking war for you and you know that. I fought my brother and argued with my mother over you because you are my woman and I'll be damned if either of them disrespect you. Especially, when you have never done anything to them." She didn't say anything.

"As your man I'm supposed to fight your battles but fuck it. You see what you want, and I'm done trying to prove no one comes before you and the kids. Yes, that's my mother and brother but you're my family too. If they can't respect you then that's where I step in. But it's all good. As long as you're happy that's the only thing that matters." She sat on the bed with her head in her hands crying. Usually I would comfort her but right now it's not happening. I needed to get out of there before I snapped and said something I would regret.

"Stan lets go." Essence was asleep on the couch and him and Sean were in the kitchen talking. She must've come after we went upstairs.

"Kane don't leave."

"Why not April?" I turned around and she stood at the top of the stairs speechless.

"Exactly. I'm out."

"Kane please."

"Fuck you April. When you're done being selfish call me. If I'm not with someone else, we may be able to rekindle whatever this is. But until then don't call me unless it has to do with my son."

"Oh so you're going to keep Lexi from me?"

"You sound real stupid. Stan lets go before I fuck around and hurt her feelings."

"Too late."

"Stop playing victim April. You don't want me so it's time for me to go." No one said a word.

"What happened that fast?" Essence woke up wiping her eyes.

"I don't know. Ever since her ex nigga came back April changed. Good luck with him beating your ass."

"Get out Kane."

"Fuck you bitch. I was already leaving."

"Hold up Kane." Stan said when I called her that. He was lucky I had respect for him otherwise we'd be in here fighting too. He knows like everyone else I hated for someone to interrupt or get in my business but she's his sister, so he got a pass. I stepped out to the car and stood there lighting a black and mild.

April pissed me off so bad all I could do was sit on the passenger side of the car with my head back and eyes closed. I understand the hormones are a problem in women when they're pregnant, but she is fully aware of what comes out of her mouth. I'm not sure if she's acting like that over my family members but one thing's for sure; if I ever see the ex nigga, he's dead on sight.

****

Two and a half weeks went by and April and I still weren't speaking. She had a doctor appointment yesterday and Essence kept me on face time the entire time. Some may call me childish but the two of us won't be in the same room until she is in labor, which is right now.

I'm pressing this elevator button hard as hell and the

85

shit still won't come. I glanced around for the stairs and took them two at a time instead. I stepped in the room and she was sitting there crying while Essence held her hand and her mom sat in the corner who's still recovering from what that fuck nigga did to her.

"Why is she crying? What happened to my son?" I started panicking.

"She's in a lot of pain Kane, that's all. She has to dilate a little more before they can give her an epidural."

"Oh." I took my jacket off and sat in the other chair next to her mom. I probably should've held her hand or something, but Essence had it. When she started pushing I would do it then.

My phone went off and I looked down and started grinning. It was this shorty I met a few days ago and the two of us had been texting one another. I thought April would come to her senses after the first week, but she didn't and then another week passed and still nothing. I said fuck it and went out.

The chick approached me and since I'm with no one we exchanged phone numbers. I heard someone suck their teeth and it was April when I looked up, but she's the one who ended us.

I hate when a chick broke it off with you but expects you to stay at home waiting on her to call. I did it for two weeks and I'm over it. Shit, Essence is the one who called me here because she still mad, but I'm over it.

"Aaahhhhhhhh it hurts mommy. I can't take this pain." Her screaming out like that made me put my phone away and go to her. Essence moved out the way and I grabbed her hand.

"Go get the doctor and tell him he better give her some fucking medicine." April laid back on the bed and I stared at her. Throughout what she's going through she was still beautiful to me.

"Ok let's see how far you are?" The doctor came in, put gloves on and checked her. She told the nurse it was time for the epidural. They had her leaned over and stuck this big ass needle in her back.

"You ok?" I asked rubbing her hair when they left.

"Yes. This boy must be ready." She squeezed my hand and I looked at her.

"What's wrong?"

"Nothing. It's just a little pressure. I thought it would hurt more."

"If you wanna hold my hand longer just ask." She sucked her teeth and turned her head. I turned her back around and leaned down to kiss her.

"You'll always be my woman regardless if we're together or not. I love you April and thank you for giving me my son."

"Kane, I…" She was about to say something, but the doctor came in, checked once more and told April it was time to push. An hour later she pushed my son out and a nigga let a tear drop. He weighed eight pounds and seven ounces. The nurses did everything they had to and handed him to me. Essence tried to hold him, but I curved her ass real quick.

"When are we going to be able to hold him?" Lexi asked with her arms folded. They came up an hour after April delivered and I still wouldn't allow anyone to touch him. I saw my mom walking in the door and I shook my head no. I handed Kane Jr. to his mother, stepped outside and pulled my mom with me.

"I guess she doesn't want me to see my grandson." My mom said rolling her eyes.

"Ma look. That is my son in there and she is his mother. If she isn't comfortable with you being around her then I'm not putting her in a position for you to act up. You will see him when he comes home."

"Kane are you serious?"

"Dead serious. You sit here and want to pretend like you didn't play a part in the way she feels. You did this to yourself when you accused and blamed her for that bullshit. If you wanna be mad, be mad at yourself."

"I see what Stacy is talking about now. You're picking her over your own blood." I had to control my anger because my mom was about to make me flip on her.

"If that's how you feel then so be it. But let me leave you with this to think about and since you two are in cahoots with each other, make sure you pass it on." I told her and escorted her to the elevator.

"April doesn't have to fuck with you because of me if

she doesn't want to. She tried to respect you and Stacy as my family but the two of you treated her like shit and talked about her and that doesn't sit right with me either."

"Kane…" She tried to speak and I cut her off.

"Ma, you know I'll never allow anyone to disrespect my family, but she is my family too and if y'all can't get along then it is what it is. My son will know who you are so there's no need to worry about it."

"So that's it?"

"Yup. I suggest the next time you come out your face accusing someone of something, you should remember that saying sorry and not meaning it will get you nowhere."

"What are you talking about?"

"You apologized to April and she was going to let it go but then she overheard you telling me to leave her alone and it was her fault."

"Well…"

"MA, STOP IT. SHE FUCKING LEFT ME BECAUSE OF YOU AND STACY. YOU KNEW HOW MUCH I LOVED HER BUT YOU WOULDN'T STOP. WHY

THE FUCK CAN'T YOU UNDERSTAND THAT THE SHIT YOU'RE DOING IS HURTING ME TOO. WHAT THE FUCK!!" I said and punched a hole in the wall. Essence, Stan and a few other people came running out.

"Kane." She grabbed my arm and I snatched away from her.

"I'm over this shit. I need a fucking break from all of you." I went back and kissed my son on the forehead.

"Kane are you ok?" April asked and I kept walking out the door without giving her a response. I'm over everybody.

Stacy

"What you want to eat for breakfast?" Lucy asked standing in front of me with nothing on but a robe. I know what people are thinking and yes, we have been sleeping together since Essence left me, but we weren't a couple.

"I'm good with whatever you make." I went in the bathroom to relieve myself and jumped in the shower. I'm supposed to meet my mom to discuss something that happened at the hospital with Kane. She called me last night but I didn't answer and she left me a voicemail crying. I'm sure she did something that made him flip on her because it's the type of person my mom is.

I finished in the bathroom, threw some clothes on and walked in the kitchen. I rented a small three-bedroom condo for my son and I. He was coming to stay with me this weekend, so I had to finish setting his room up. I had a room for Lexi too because most likely her ass will be here too. Those two never slept out without the other one. I had Lucy buy girl stuff for her room, but she came back with some Disney shit Lexi would definitely complain about. She's already grown, and I can hear her now saying it's too kiddish for her.

After I ate, Lucy told me she was going to the mall to pick some things up. I gave her money and walked out the door. She and I were not a couple, but she did satisfy my sexual needs since Essence left me. I could've gotten it elsewhere but fuck it. If she was right here, then why not? I'm sure once everyone found out they'll talk shit, and I didn't care.

Stan knew where she was and has spoken to her on the phone but he won't come here. I'm assuming him wanting to kill her has passed because he could've done it already.

I parked at my moms' house and used my key to go in. My dad looked at me and shook his head. He let my ass have it the day Kane and I got into it. I spoke to him and continued in the house to find my mom. She was sitting at the table going through old photos of Kane and me.

"What's up ma?" I kissed her cheek and she wiped her eyes.

"I messed up Stacy."

"What are you talking about?" I grabbed a plate, put a piece of chocolate cake on it and sat next to her. My mom made the best cakes and I could never get enough.

"April had the baby last night." I didn't say anything.

"I tried to go see him and Kane wouldn't allow me in the room." I gave my mom a look asking why she went up there.

"Ma, I'm going to be honest with you. If I were Kane, I wouldn't allow you in either." She sucked her teeth.

"I'm saying. Why do you think he would allow you anywhere around April?"

"I wasn't there to see her trifling ass."

"That's exactly why you can't see your grandson. Kane loves that woman and you know how he feels about someone disrespecting her. He would never let her speak to you the way you spoke to her, nor would he sit around listening to her bash you. Ma, you put him in a predicament where he has to choose his family or you."

"I am his mother."

"And she is his woman and the mother of his kids." She gave me the side eye.

"Say what you want but she is Lexi's mom and had a hand in raising her too. You of all people should respect her more for doing that alone." My mom was stubborn as hell.

"Well, they're not together anymore. She left him because you and I put a strain on their relationship, and I say good riddance."

"Damn." Is all I could say. I knew just like everyone else knew how in love he is with April. The two of them were perfect together so to hear they weren't a couple had me feeling bad. I know what he and I went through had something to do with it too.

I've heard Essence and April speak many of times about not being with someone who has a family member they can't get along with. They felt tension would be felt at any family event and they never wanted that.

"Oh well. Kane said I could see the baby when he brought him over here." She stood up and gathered all the photos and put them in a bag.

My mom had a problem when it came to taking pictures of us when we were young. She had tons and tons of them, that she had to keep them in bags because my dad didn't want a thousand photo albums around the house.

"Your mother is who she is but you need to go make it right with your brother." My father said as I was on my way out.

"Pops, he didn't have to hit me. Yea, I may have been wrong but come on."

"Stacy will you listen to yourself. You're blaming everything on him instead of taking responsibility for your part in this. He came by to get you away from a woman you were supposed to be madly in love with but put your hands on. Then you accuse him of not being there for you. He left his family unprotected to make sure you were ok and didn't go to jail." I put my head down.

"MY FUCKING GRANDAUGHTER WAS RAPED AND THAT NIGGA IS STILL ROAMING THE STREETS STACY. WHAT TYPE OF SHIT DO YOU AND YOUR MOTHER THINK HE'S GOING THROUGH? HUH? That shit still had me feeling bad when Kane brought it up. My dad was raising his voice and it let me know he was pissed.

"You didn't think about anyone but yourself and then you get mad because his girl's mom was shot and he wanted to go be with her. I'm not sure what is going on with you and your mom, but this shit has to get fixed. My son won't even visit me over something I don't have anything to do with."

"Pops."

"No Stacy. Don't apologize to me. You and your mother both need to say that shit to Kane." I looked at him because he hated to curse.

"Your mother told me how he punched a hole in the wall and stormed out the hospital and I can tell you this. If anything happens to my son because of the shit you two are putting him through; let's just say your old man won't have anyone stopping him from fucking you up and leaving your mother."

"You would leave me." My mom came in the room crying when she heard him say that.

"Yes. I've told you before about your mouth and hateful ways to people; especially, April. That girl did nothing to you and if my son loves her then you should too. I swear you two are a fucking trip. I need to leave before I say some hurtful shit to both of you." My dad got up, snatched his keys and slammed the door on his way out.

I left my parents' house and drove over to Kane's to see if he was home but his car wasn't in the driveway. I'm assuming he was back at the hospital with his son.

At first, I thought about going up there but that most likely wasn't a good idea. Instead of waiting for the weekend, I went and picked my son up today.

Essence came to the door dressed in some yoga pants and a tank top with a sports bra under. Her body is definitely banging, and I felt my man waking up. She stood in the doorway not saying anything. This is the first time we saw or spoke to one another since I left her at April's mother house. I sent her messages to check on my son but that was it.

"SJ, your dad is here." She stepped aside for me to come in.

"Essence, I know you don't wanna hear shit from me, but I am really sorry about everything. I love you to death and when you said you were leaving me, I couldn't take it and snapped. You know I would never lay my hands on you." She didn't respond but all the tears leaving her face let me know she heard me.

"Dad, what are you doing here and why is mommy crying? Ma, what's wrong?"

"Uh ah, uncle Stacy what did you do?" Lexi asked standing in front of Essence with her hands on her hips. I loved how they protected her and didn't care that it was me who did it and said how they felt.

"I'm ok you two." She wiped her face and leaned down to kiss them on the cheek.

"Your dad is taking you until Monday."

"Why?" SJ asked her.

"It's Thursday SJ and I wanted an extra day with you that's all."

"You could've had everyday with me had you not messed up." He said and ran up the steps. I never thought about how my stupid choices would affect my son not being around me every day.

"I'll talk to him uncle Stacy, but I have to say one thing." She walked up on me.

"You made my dad and aunty Essence mad. I'm not sure how you're going to fix it, but you better hurry up. I need my mom and dad to get back together and SJ wants the same for you two." She said using her finger to point to Essence and me. I loved my niece, but she is too much sometimes. Essence told her it was enough and sent her to pack a bag.

"I love you Essence." I moved closer and hugged her.

"Stacy please."

"You don't miss me." She didn't say anything as I placed kisses on her neck.

"Sssss." She moaned out quietly. I knew her body better than she did and knew where each one of her spots were.

"Do you miss me Essence?" She nodded her head yes and put her hands around my neck. The two of us kissed one another and I pushed her against the wall gently.

"The kids Stacy." She whispered in my ear. I checked the door and made sure it was locked and took her down in the man cave. I locked the door too and stripped her out of the clothes she had on.

"Damn, I missed you." I said and had her sit on my pool table. I got on my knees and sucked on her pussy until she begged me to stop. She wanted to give me head, but I wanted to feel inside her.

"Shittttt baby. You still feel good. Fuck, I'm about to cum already." She didn't say anything as I came in two minutes. She sat on my lap and wound her hips to wake me back up. Essence definitely had a limp when she walked but it didn't affect her ability to fuck me well at any time.

"I love you Stacy." She moaned in my ear when she came from riding me. I smacked her on the ass and pounced her up and down harder.

"Cum for me again Essence." She grabbed on to the back of the chair that we moved to and rode the hell out of me.

"Fuckkkkk baby. Essence make me cum again." She slipped her tongue in my mouth and brought me to a release. I had to hold her tight just to make sure she didn't move. I planned on getting her pregnant again. Say what you want but she and I will be together again.

"Stacy, I'm not on birth control." She laid her head on my shoulder.

"I know." She lifted her head and stared at me.

"I know it's going to take time to get over what I did to you but Essence you are and will be the only woman I love. You are the mother of my son and the baby I just put inside you." She laughed and threw her head back.

"I'm going to do everything I can to win you back baby. I swear I am." My head was on her chest as we were still in the same position with her on top.

"You have to start by getting rid of Lucy."

"Huh?"

"I know you're over there fucking her." She lifted herself off me and went in the bathroom down here and turned the water on to wash up.

"Done." I didn't ask how she knew because I didn't care. If she's willing to give me another chance I'm doing anything she asks.

"Stacy, I will give you another chance because I really believe you are truly sorry. I also know how much you love me and your son but I'm telling you if she interferes in any way, I will never fuck with you again."

"I won't mess up Essence. You have no idea how bad I've been waiting for you to take me back." She looked at me crazy.

"Don't look at me like that. She may be satisfying my sexual needs, but she doesn't do me like you." Now she was confused.

"Essence, you are the only woman who can make me say her name during sex. You take care of our son and you never complain. You own my mind and another woman will never be able to say she has me the way you do."

"Better not be." I hugged her and we finished getting ourselves together in the bathroom. We opened the door and SJ and Lexi were standing there grinning.

"Hmph. I guess mommy threw it on you again huh?" SJ said and started laughing.

"What are you talking about?"

"Dad, we heard you making noise and don't say it was mommy because she doesn't sound like that."

"Yea. My daddy makes those same noises sometimes when him and mommy are having grown up time. You do know that means you're whipped." Lexi said and I chased her around the damn living room. I missed the hell out of how we used to play around with the kids.

"I'll be back tomorrow to take you out on a date."

"Really."

"I'm going to make you fall back in love with me Essence. I don't want you to think sex is all I want from you. I want all of you again."

"I'm still in love with you and I'll be ready. You just be ready to be to make love to me all night." She whispered in my ear as the kids got in the car.

"You know I'm ready for that. I love you."

"I love you too and don't forget to handle that. You know thing one and thing two will tell me if you don't." She pointed to the kids.

"You want me to do it in front of them?" I asked her about getting rid of Lucy.

"No fool. But I'm sure when you tell her she'll pop up." She laughed and shut the door.

The kids and I went to Fun time America and stayed there for a few hours. I took them to the movies afterwards and then to my house because it was after nine and they both were tired. The two of them took showers and went to their room to get dressed. I sent a text to Lucy and told her it was over and that she had to stay with her brother from now on.

Essence may be giving me another chance but I'm not going to rush and move back in until she's ready. Lucy and I went back and forth arguing over the text because she claimed it wasn't over. I shut my phone off and hopped in the shower and stayed in there for at least a half hour.

****

105

"Get your hands off me." I thought I heard Lucy's voice but there's no way she's here. The kids were in the bed, so I know they didn't open the door but then again, she had a key. I threw some sweats on and ran downstairs.

"What the fuck?" I yelled out. Lexi had Lucy by the hair on the ground while SJ sat there laughing with his phone videotaping it. Don't ask me how the hell it happened.

"Stacy, get these bad ass kids."

"What happened?" I pulled Lexi off her but it took me a few minutes because her grip was tight as hell.

"I was sitting on the couch waiting for you and she came out of nowhere pulling my hair." Lucy stood up fixing her clothes and trying to pat down her hair.

"Ok. But how did you get on the ground?" SJ and Lexi were behind me cracking up and it was hard as hell not to laugh with them.

"Her and your son. He tripped me when I stood up and she grabbed my hair again and started smacking me. What the hell are those bitches teaching them?" Lexi hit her in the face with a tennis ball that was on the ground. I have no idea where it even came from. It hit her in the eye and she started screaming.

"Yo, take your ass upstairs." I told both of them.

"Wait." SJ said and walked over to where Lucy was with Lexi on his heels.

"What?" Lucy tried to get tough with them.

"Don't bring your ass over here anymore. He and my mom are back together."

"Yea. Beat it bitch." Lexi kicked her hard as hell in the leg.

"I swear to God I'm about to kill them kids." The minute she said that, I lifted her up by the shirt and tossed her out the house. She went tumbling down the steps. I slammed the door and went looking for those bad motherfuckers.

"SJ give me your phone. Your ass is on punishment from it and the game and Lexi you know what your father is going to do."

"He's not going to do anything because all he's worried about is some new woman he's seeing." She said and stepped out the room. I wasn't sure what she meant by that, so I asked

SJ and he told me ever since he and April broke up he's been going out with some lady.

They were at the mall and supposedly ran into them there. I may not be speaking to my brother but if he's doing it like that he foul as hell. He should wait a few months before he takes Lexi to meet someone but that's none of my business.

Essence

I was hysterical laughing watching the video of Lexi grabbing that bitch Lucy hair and smacking her. When she threw the tennis ball in her eye, I swear I peed on myself a little. I know it isn't right to laugh but if anyone saw the video they would too.

Kane and Stan found out about it because SJ sent them the video thinking they would find it funny, but they were pissed. Lexi is on punishment and can't come over for two weeks and Stacy told SJ he lost his phone and video games for a week. He only videotaped it so he didn't get in as much trouble. I wasn't going to punish him at all but his father said he couldn't let it go because regardless she is a grown up.

I know he's probably wondering how I found out about him and that trick. Fortunately, for me, my best friend told me she overheard Stan going off about Stacy not only keeping her in a hotel but then shacking up with her in a condo he purchased.

At first I was upset because in my eyes it meant he wasn't going to fight to try and win me back and that hurt like hell. The day he came apologizing I was in my feelings and knew the way he said it this time, he really meant it. Yea, he said it the night it happened, but it could've been because he didn't wanna let go. After he hugged me my body succumbed to everything else he did right after and before you knew it the two of us were having sex.

It's going to be different with him trying to take me out on a date but at the same time it's like he was courting me all over again and a bitch couldn't help but get butterflies.

The day of our date I had him drop the kids off to his mom's so I could get ready. I got my nails, hair and feet done, along with a massage to relieve all the stress. He picked me up in a brand-new Chrysler 200s and the shit was nice as hell. He told me it was mine and if I didn't want it we could get something else. He wined, dined and made love to me all night and I felt like we grew closer. I loved that man and this is the only time he's ever messed up.

I gave him a second chance because in all honesty he

did love his family and he also had a good heart. Lucy may have had him look out for her, but she will never come before his son or me. He's made that clear to her on more than one occasion and her ass wasn't happy about it.

****

Today, April was bringing home the baby but she was staying with her mom at her boyfriends' house. Kane wasn't too happy, but they weren't together, and he was kicking it with some other chick. When April told me that I felt bad because she wanted Kane back but after finding out he moved on she said forget it.

I got to the hospital and Kane was sitting in the chair holding his son. April came out the bathroom walking slowly. You could tell he still loved her and vice versa but neither of them spoke on it. Kane put the baby's snowsuit on and placed him in the car seat.

"Alright lil man. I'll be by one day this week." He kissed him on the cheek and stared at April who turned her head.

"Get them there safe." He told me and stepped out the room.

"April why are you doing him like that? You know that man loves you."

"What am I supposed to say? Essence he has someone else now. You think I don't want to be with him? I fucking miss him like crazy but he doesn't want me anymore." She sat on the bed and started crying.

"What you crying for?" We both jumped when we heard Kane's voice.

"Oh nothing. Must be postpartum on something." She wiped her eyes and stood up to get the rest of her things together.

"Oh. You better get that checked out. I left my phone." He reached on the windowsill, grabbed it, kissed the baby again and left.

"April why didn't you say anything?"

"No need to. I'm ready to go." I felt bad for her but I'm done trying to help her. He won't know how she feels unless she opens her mouth and I can't make her do it.

The doctor gave her the discharge papers and a nurse came in with a wheelchair. She sat down and I attached Kane Jr.'s car seat to the stroller and pushed him out. We got downstairs and saw Kane and some woman walking to the front door. I know damn well he wasn't that damn disrespectful to have a woman waiting for him while he visited his newborn.

April grabbed my arm and asked me not to say anything and it burned me up. She asked the nurse to stop walking and we watched the two of them walk to his car. He leaned down and kissed her on the cheek, but you saw her grab his face and engage him into a more passionate one.

"Isn't he your son's father?" The nurse asked being messy.

"Yes it is. We aren't together so it's fine." April is a better bitch then me. I would've cursed her out and let Kane have it too.

I left her with the nurse and baby to get my car. Kane and the chick stopped kissing and she wiped his lips with her finger. He looked up and noticed me standing there and all I could do was shake my head.

"Essence hold up." I continued walking, not trying to get caught in the middle but it was hard not to.

"What's up?"

"Where's my son?" He didn't ask for her. Maybe he is done with her so I decided not to say anything.

"They're coming down now. I came out to pull the car around."

"Oh ok. Essence what you saw." I turned around and stared at him.

"It doesn't matter what I saw. You aren't my man nor are you Aprils'. You are free to do what you want but you could've had the decency to flaunt your chick around elsewhere and not where the mother of your son just gave birth at."

"I know and it wasn't planned. After I left you two, she was downstairs leaving from visiting someone too."

"She's the new woman in your life now?"

"We're just friends. She wants more and…"

"Let me guess, you're not ready right."

"I was gonna say she's too clingy and once she got the dick it got worst. To be honest she probably followed me

114

here." My mouth hit the floor.

"What you think I don't know you're interrogating me for your friend? Come on Essence. I'm no fool. When you run back and tell April what you saw if she didn't witness it herself, remind her that this is the decision she made. I waited two weeks for her to get out that funk and come back to me but she didn't."

"You didn't waste any time."

"Just like she didn't waste any time speaking to that nigga on the phone or meeting up with him." I had no idea what he spoke of.

"Yea. I see you didn't know either. Your friend is sneaky, but she needs to remember or maybe you should tell her who I am."

"Kane, she loves you." He threw his head back laughing like I told a joke.

"Nah. She loves her ex. If she didn't, the day she met up with him after her mom was shot, she would've called and let me take him out."

"What are you talking about?" His phone rang and he

looked down at it smirking.

"Ask your friend what she was doing two days after she broke up with me. I have to go. Shorty wants some dick."

"I thought you said she's clingy."

"She is but she has some good pussy." He chucked up the deuces and went back to his car.

I started my car and drove around to pick April and the baby up. Of course, she asked what took me so long, but I didn't answer. The nurse strapped the baby in the back and I broke the stroller down to put in my trunk. As bad as a bitch wanted to ask what she was doing with Demetrius I didn't say anything. I'm not happy about what Kane is doing but I understand. Who visits with the guy that tried to kill your mom, punched you in the face while you were pregnant and basically kidnapped you? April had her priorities messed up and if she doesn't get it together Kane will never take her back.

We parked in the driveway where she would be staying, and her mom opened the door smiling. We all grabbed everything and went inside. Her mom took the baby out and held him. April went to the room and I followed her with every intention of yelling at her, but she went to the bathroom. My phone rang from an unknown number and usually I ignored those but today I didn't.

"Hello."

"Hi. Is this Essence umm." The person said on the phone. Instead of waiting for her to guess my last name I just told her yes.

"This is Riverview Medical center. Do you know someone by the name of Stacy?" I didn't even allow her to finish.

"Yes, that's my fiancé."

"Oh ok. Can you come to the hospital?"

"For what? What happened to him?"

"I can't tell you over the phone, but you should get down here fast."

I hung the phone up and told April I would be back. She asked me what happened, but I couldn't give her an answer. I called Stacy's mom and told her what the hospital told me and she said they would meet us at the hospital. I was skeptical about calling Kane so I didn't.

I ran in the hospital and to the nurses' station panting and trying to catch my breath. Stacy's parents came in a few minutes later and asked what happened. We sat there listening to the nurse tell us he had been brought in with a gunshot wound to his stomach. They had him surgery at the moment and would tell us more later. I knew then Kane had to be told what happened. I picked my phone up to call and it rang then went to voicemail.

"Kane your brother got shot and he's still in surgery. When you get this message, we're at Riverview hospital. I'll call you back when I hear something." I hung the phone up and leaned my head on Stacy's mom shoulder. She ran her hand over my head and told me it would be ok. I didn't understand why she was so nice to me but hated April. I planned on asking her one day, but not today.

Kane

"Suck all that shorty." I grabbed the back of her hair and pumped harder in her mouth. She didn't do a good job in giving head, but her pussy was decent enough for me to stay around.

"Lay down." I pulled my dick out because she could never make me cum giving me oral sex. She always complained that she wanted to make me feel good, but it never happened during oral sex. I opened her legs, slid the condom on and pounded away. The entire time April stayed on my mind.

"Fuck Kane. I'm cumming again." Her legs started shaking and a few minutes later she came all over her sheets. I flipped her over and plunged into her from the back and once again April invaded my mind. I'm sure it was my conscience telling me I had no business here, when she's where my heart and mind was but fuck it.

"I'm cumming shorty." I pulled out, took the condom off and squirted all over her back. I smacked her ass and walked in the bathroom. She came behind me and wrapped her arms around my waist.

"Can I take a shower over here?" She nodded her head yes and tried to get in with me but I told her hell no. I may fuck bitches but certain things I only do with my woman and showering with a random ain't happening, even if it is her place.

"Kane, your phone is ringing." She yelled in the bathroom.

"Who is it?"

"Someone named April." I smiled because she finally called me.

"Answer it."

"Are you sure?" I told her yea and you could hear her answering the questions April asked. I'm assuming it's *where is Kane* and *who are you* because she said in the shower and then her name.

"Ok, I'll tell him." She said and hung the phone up. I shut the shower off and she handed me a towel to dry off.

"She said something happened but obviously you were too busy to answer your phone. Also, that you aren't shit and don't have to worry about her contacting you ever again. When you want to see the baby call someone named Essence to set it up." I nodded my head to pretend it didn't bother me but it did.

I threw my clothes on and told shorty I would see her later. I sat in my car and looked at my phone trying to decide if it's a good idea to call her back. There was another missed call from April and a few from Essence, which was weird. There's a voicemail notification as well.

My blue tooth was hooked up to my car so when Essence said Stacy got shot a nigga hauled ass to the hospital. We may not be speaking but that damn sure didn't mean anyone had the right to try and take his life.

"Kane thank goodness you're here." My mom said and tried to give me a hug, but I moved past her to ask my dad what happened. The look on my moms' face was priceless but she made me this way to her. He had me take a walk with him outside and explained that Stacy was going in his house and someone did a drive by. No one knows anything else but the doctor just left and said he'll be fine." He looked at me and asked how I been.

"Look son, you two may not be speaking but you are still my son and I don't appreciate you putting me in the middle."

"Pops it's not like that."

"Kane, I let your mother and brother have it already. I'm not going to stand here and say you need to talk to them because I'm not sure after what they did, I would be able to either. But don't leave me out hanging over it. My grandson hasn't even met me yet and you know I'm not happy about it." He and I spoke for a few more minutes and went back inside. I told Essence I would pick the kids up and take them with me so she could stay.

A few days went by and the kids and I did everything under the sun as far as going places. We were driving to the mall when the girl Tasia I was messing with asked me to stop by. Now usually, I wouldn't introduce my daughter to someone that's not my woman but she's seen her before at the mall, so

Lexi was fully aware of who she is. They didn't have to get out the car and we weren't staying long.

I hit her up and told her we were outside. As we sat there waiting for her to come out Lexi claimed she had to use the bathroom. We walked up the steps and Tasia opened the door damn near naked and SJ's eyes almost popped out his head.

"Daddy why she dressed like that?" Lexi asked and I stood in front of Tasia and told her to put some clothes on.

"I'm not sure but hurry up so we could go. Tasia, my daughter needs to use the bathroom. Is that ok?" She nodded her head yes. I shut the door and went to her bedroom.

"I'm sorry Kane. I didn't know the kids were with you." She stood on her tippy toes and tried to kiss me but I turned my head.

"You let me kiss you at the hospital." I laughed because little did she know I knew April was watching. I heard them talking when they came off the elevator and didn't turn around.

"What did you call me over here for?" I asked looking down on my phone.

"What I wanted can't happen because the kids are here." Honestly, my dick wasn't hard or craving her pussy, so it didn't really matter how horny she was.

"Nah. But let me use the bathroom right quick and I'll come back later when the kids go to bed." She nodded her head and started putting some clothes on. I came out the bathroom and heard the kids talking to her.

"He's only using you until my mommy takes him back."

"Oh yea." I heard Tasia say. First off who continues a conversation with a kid?

"Yea. See my mommy has my daddy making noises when they have adult time. Do you? Because if you don't it means you're not doing a good job."

"Yo Lexi. Apologize right now before I beat your ass." She did what I said and the two of them waited for me by the door.

"Uhmmm ok then." Tasia said looking like she is about to cry.

"What's wrong?"

"Is that true? I mean you don't make any noise when we have sex."

"Mannnn. I'm not about to discuss any sexual relations I've had with other women. Why the hell are you having a conversation or better yet allowing her to say that to you."

"Kane, she's your daughter. What do I look like disciplining someone else's kid?"

"I'm not saying disciplining her. I'm saying changing the subject or something." I walked away from her and told those badass kids to go to the car. I watched them get in and turned around to see Tasia with no clothes on. I shook my head in disgust because she really thought I would leave them out in the car to fuck her.

"Five minutes Kane." She leaned back on the couch and started playing with herself. I closed the door and left her in that exact position. I may play a lot of games but doing some shit like that is a no go in my book.

"I'm telling you two right now that if I ever hear you talking that grown up shit again, I'm beating both of y'all ass."

They put their head down. Everyone else may get a kick out of that shit but I damn sure didn't.

****

A week went by and Stacy was up and moving around a little at the hospital, but I hadn't gone up there yet. Tasia and I were spending a little time together and yea she was clingy but she kept my mind off of what was going on right now.

Essence called and asked me to come up right away but wouldn't tell me is anything was wrong. Something in my gut told me to drop shorty off but then that would take me out twenty minutes to do that and then another twenty to get back. I said fuck it, and had her come with me.

We got off the floor and went to room my brother was in and he sat up when I came in. He looked good for someone who got shot a week ago. I heard some heels behind me and turned around to see my baby momma looking fly as fuck. Her snap back game from having my son had her looking like she didn't just give birth.

April had on some black fitted jeans with some red bottoms on her feet. She wore a sweater that hung off her

126

shoulder and she wore some diamond studs in her ear that were huge. Her hair was pulled to the side and her lip-gloss was popping. A nigga ain't gonna lie, she was a bad bitch and all I wanted to do was snatch her clothes off and fuck the shit out of her.

"Hello Kane."

"What up?" I said and licked my lips. She smirked, moved past me and stopped when she saw Tasia and my mom in the corner talking. This is the first time they met and I know my mother was being petty but I wasn't going to address it right now. She turned around to look at me and I shrugged my shoulders.

"Why did you call me here Essence?" My mom looked up at Essence with an attitude.

"I asked her to call you and Kane up here April. I didn't know he had anyone with him." Stacy said and asked her to move close to him.

"April, I just wanna say I'm sorry for the way I treated you. I was in my feelings about Essence leaving me and took it out on you. You've been best friends with her before me and I can see how it's interfering with your friendship. When I say that, I mean you don't come to the house, you only call her cell and I haven't met my nephew yet. I swear that shit won't ever happen again."

"Mommy are you coming home now?" Lexi asked and hopped off my dad's lap.

"No sweetie, but you know you're more than welcome to stay with me."

"Why wouldn't that be a given to stay with her so called mom?" My mother mumbled but I heard it and my blood was boiling.

"Grandma Brown would love to see you and SJ."

"I want to see my brother daddy. I'm going home with mommy."

"Dag Lexi. You're just going to leave me."

"Daddy all you do is spend time with her and I don't like her."

"LEXI. You apologize right now to her." Lexi walked over to Tasia and did what April told her. Damn, she had Lexi in check, and I loved that shit.

"Kane you're going to allow her to speak to Lexi like that?" My mother asked.

"That's her daughter. Why wouldn't I?"

"We all know she's not Lexi's mom." I could see April's eyes getting watery when she said it. Not only was she foul for saying it but she brought it up in front of Tasia.

"Yo ma." April put her hand up and walked over to her. I went to stand next to her because these two weren't going to fight even though my mom deserved it.

"You can say what you want but she's my daughter. I may not have birthed her but that is me all day."

"A mother wouldn't allow what happened to her, happen."

"Don't you dare bring that up in front of her." I looked at Lexi and she was crying.

"I can say what I want." My mom stood and took her earrings off like she was ready to fight. The scene in front of me was crazy.

"You are a hateful woman and the way you're treating me is nothing compared to what Lexi is probably feeling from

129

you bringing that dreadful shit up. I can tell you right now you will never, and I repeat never meet my son. I don't need you filling his head up with bullshit like you've been doing Lexi." My mom didn't say anything.

"Oh, you don't want Kane to know that you called me a whore and wanna get my son tested. Or the fact you told Lexi it was my fault the man did those horrible things to her."

"Ma, I know you didn't say any shit like that." Stacy said because I was at a loss for words not knowing what to say after hearing my mom was doing it.

"I feel the way I feel, so what? And as far as seeing your son, I don't need to. This young woman right here just told me she can't wait to give Kane a baby. You're nothing but a whore who slept with my son when you knew he had a woman. Yea. Sherri told me how you stole her away from him." That must've been the straw that broke the camel's back because April smacked the shit out of my mom, and no one moved. My mom went to swing back and my dad pulled her away.

"Yo calm the fuck down." I said to April when I pulled her in the hallway.

"Get the fuck off me Kane. This is all your fault."

"How is this my fault April? I didn't know she was going to say that shit or that she told Lexi those things."

"I guess you wouldn't being you're so wrapped up in your friend."

"April don't start." She pushed me off her and started walking away.

"You know I met with Demetrius a few days after we broke up to find out any information, he would give me about Glenn. I planned on telling you the little bit he did give me, but you couldn't get your head out your ass long enough to check on me those two weeks." She was disappointed in me and had every right.

"Yes, I broke up with you but I was pregnant. PREGNANT KANE. Not once did you ask me how I was doing or of I needed anything. You know what? It doesn't even matter anymore." She said pressing the elevator button. I felt like shit because I didn't check on her and here, I thought she

131

tried to get back with her ex and the entire time she wanted to help me get the dude who violated Lexi.

"What doesn't matter?"

"Us Kane. We don't matter. I came here knowing you would be here to tell you everything and ask you to come home but I see it was a mistake. Go enjoy your life with your new baby mother." I ran over to her, hopped on the elevator and pushed her against the wall.

"April." I kissed on her neck.

"It's over Kane. I'm never fucking with you again." I backed up from her and stared to see if she meant what she said and sure enough there was pain and hurt in her eyes. That told me she was really done with a nigga and I couldn't take it. I felt like my brother did when Essence left him.

"Go home and think about what you're saying. I may be fucking her but you and I will never be over."

"Fuck you Kane. You're not going to scare me into being with you. I don't want you and the faster you get it through your head, the better. Leave me the fuck alone." She pushed me back on the elevator and left. The doors closed and I stood there stuck.

I went back in the room and my mom had the nerve to ask me if I hit April for hitting her. Lexi was sitting on Essence lap crying and SJ laid in the bed with Stacy. Everything that went down probably could've been avoided had my mom not been so fucking petty and childish. My dad was shaking his head and Tasia sat there looking scared to death.

I told Lexi to come with me but she asked Essence if she could go home with her instead. My mom got up to leave and Lexi went to where she was.

"Nana, why would you say those things to my mom?" My mother bent down to her.

"That's not your mother Lexi."

"Stop saying that nana. You may not like her but she is my mom. She is the only one who wanted me when my biological mom didn't. She didn't even know my dad and still loved and took care of me. And she would never let that man hurt me so can you please stop saying that?"

"Lexi."

"No nana. I don't know this lady my dad is with and you told her my business. I know you may not like April but why did you have to make me remember what he did to me?" She started crying and my mom looked at me. I picked her up and she cried on my shoulder.

"Let's go Tasia." We walked downstairs to my car and neither of us said a word.

"I'll talk to you later." I told her when I dropped her off at home. I drove to my house and packed some clothes for Lexi. I know she missed April and it wasn't right that no one took her there. I tried calling April to tell her I was bringing her but she had her phone off.

"Hey Kane. April just got here. She's in the shower." Ms. Brown said when she opened the door.

I carried Lexi up to the room her mom told me to put her in and laid her down on the bed. I went to the room where April was, and my son had just woken up. I changed his diaper and took him downstairs to ask Ms. Brown where his bottles were. She handed me one and I sat in the rocking chair and fed him. Looking down at my son made me smile. He was a spitting image of me, and my mom was mad as hell she couldn't see him. That's why she said the dumb shit about needing a test.

"Kane, when he's done eating, burp him and bring him back upstairs. I'm going to bed." April said and turned around leaving me there in my thoughts. I did what she said and took him up to where she was. She was lying in the bed and I could hear her sniffling. My mother said some fucked up shit to her and at this moment I realized the fighting would most likely continue. The two of us were better off leaving each other alone. I walked out the room and didn't say anything.

I got in my car and drove home and shed some tears of my own. I loved the fuck out of April, but we couldn't be together.

April

I thought having a baby with Kane and being his fiancé would make my life complete. We had Lexi, a house, a baby on the way and each other. But his mother ruined it for us and now a bitch is miserable as hell.

Every time I looked at my son, I found myself crying because he looked just like him. Lexi had been with me every day since he dropped her off three weeks ago. She and I have been stuck like glue and SJ wasn't happy. Essence ended up bringing him over here two days ago because he was tired of being home alone. I hated taking the ride every day to drop them off at school but it was worth it so I could see her.

"Fuck him April. Let's go out." Essence had been asking me every weekend to go out. Now that my ex had someone new, I didn't want to run into them together. Honestly, I didn't want to go anywhere but my mom took the kids with her and her man to some cabin overnight. Kane wasn't too happy because he felt Kane Jr. was too young but I told him it was only for the night and he agreed.

Yes, I made sure to include him about his son but through text messages only. When he came to the house to see him four to five times a week, I would lock myself in my room. I was having a very hard time dealing with the break up even though I'm the one who initiated it.

"Fine Essence. I'll meet you there around eleven." I told her about the club that just opened up last month. It was new and people were bragging about it on face book.

I went in my closet and took out a white bodycon dress I ordered offline and some silver Medallion heels from Versace. They were bad as hell and I had to have them. Kane kept my bank account full and put money in there every week and I wasn't complaining. I did spoil myself here and there.

Actually, I was happy because I have been looking for my own place down here by my mom. She didn't mind us staying with her but we still needed our own privacy.

"Damn bitch. You're about to shut shit down in this outfit." Essence said when she met me at the door.

"Girl bye." I waved her off and we went inside. She said there was a VIP spot with our name on it and when we stepped in, I almost came on myself. Kane sat there looking so damn good I wanted to take him in the bathroom and let him do bad things to me. He didn't notice me so we moved passed him and I felt someone grab my hand. I turned around and it was some dude with dreads. He was sexy as hell too but I'm not looking for anyone, so I kept it moving. We sat on the couch and I glanced over to where Kane was he was staring at me.

"Why didn't you tell me he would be here?"

"Because if I did, you wouldn't have come. Girl forget him. Enjoy yourself." She said and we both took a shot of the Remy the waitress brought over. After a few more drinks we decided to go on the dance floor.

Do you mind if I talk to you?

Do you mind if I touch you there?

Now you know you can't do better baby,

I know that it don't get no better than me.

Do you mind was playing in the background as I

danced in a zone next to Essence who was grinding all over Stacy. I hadn't even realized he was there. I felt some hands on my waist and didn't bother to turn around because I could smell him. Kane wore the same cologne every day and it turned me on every time.

He kissed on my neck and I let my hand go around his and grinded on him. I could feel his man rising and a bitch got turned all the way on. The Back to sleep remix came on and Kane started singing it in my ear making me wetter than I already was.

"Really Kane?" I heard some chick say but refused to turn around. He wasn't here with me so whatever they had going on is his problem.

"Go ahead with that Tasia." He said still dancing with me.

"I'm tired of this bitch." I heard her say and turned around.

"Look Tasia." I stared her up and down and saw jealousy written on her face.

"I didn't ask your man to come dance with me nor did I

know he came with you. If you want him, take him, but there's no need to call me out my name. We're not friends and I don't owe you shit. He is my kids' father; nothing more, nothing less."

"Bitch you only have one kid with him. Stop claiming the girl because she ain't yours." I was so over people telling me Lexi wasn't mine. I knew that, just like she knew, but the adoption would be going through any day now. See people were unaware Kane and I started the process not too long ago and were waiting on the judge to finalize the paperwork.

"Kane you better get her."

"Nah. I'm tired of everybody saying that shit to you. Handle your business baby." He kissed me on the cheek and stepped back. I moved closer to her and punched her in the face and only stopped when someone picked me up. Essence and I fucked that girl up. We weren't into jumping bitches but anyone could get it when it came to them talking about the kids. Security had to call the ambulance for her because that's how bad we did her.

"Kane what are you doing?" I asked when he placed me

in his car. He handed me my purse and phone and got in on the driver's side. I didn't say anything as he drove and pulled up at his house; well our old house.

"Get out." I refused to move so he took me out and threw me over his shoulder. He opened the door, locked it and put me down when we made it to his room. He sat on the bed in front of me and sparked a blunt.

"Dance for me." He hit the remote on the television and put on music. The crazy shit is Keri Hilson's song *Slow Dance* came on. The same one I danced for him at his welcome home party. He smirked which let me know he had that shit set up somehow.

"Why?" I asked turning around in front of him so he could unzip my dress.

"Because I love that shit." My dress hit the floor and he smiled. I had on a pair of black thongs and a black sheer bra to match. My shoes were still on and the song played loud on the sound bar.

Make this moment last forever baby,

your body's calling me,

I don't, want to, come on, too strong, but something

happens when we slow dance.

The music continued playing as he watched, and I swear he didn't blink. I put my foot on the bed, next to him and he ran his hands up and down my leg. I let my hands roam my neck and then my body in a sexual way that had him rock hard.

"I have the baddest baby momma in the world. Come here." He pulled me close and gave me a shotgun from the blunt and then our tongues played together for what seemed like forever.

"Take everything else off except those shoes." I did like he asked and instead of waiting for him to lay me down I stood in front of him, spread my legs and bent all the way down.

"Damn baby. She wet as hell." He ran his fingers up and down my slit then replaced it with his tongue. I came instantly and one would think he would stop but he kept going until my body finally gave out on the fourth orgasm and had me almost fall over.

"Still taste good." I stood him up and removed his shirt. He kicked his shoes off and I took his jeans and boxers off. My best friend stood at attention and I'll be damned if I didn't handle that.

"April fuck. You're going to make me cum already." I made it sloppy and let his dick touch the back of my throat. I made a humming sound and he lost all control and came.

"What do you want tonight April?" He asked as I stroked his man and stuck my tongue in his mouth.

"I just want you Kane. I want you to make my body feel good as only you can. You think you can do that for me?"

"I'll do whatever you want baby." He lifted me up and tossed me against the wall forcefully but not like he was angry. He entered me and we both moaned out like it was our first time.

"I miss the fuck out of you April." He said fucking the hell out of me against the wall.

"I miss you too baby. I'm lost without you. Oh shittttt Kane. Here I cum baby. Here I cummmmmm." I let go and he looked down grinning. He always got cocky when he could get me that wet. He laid me down on the bed and stared in my eyes as he stroked me slowly.

"Is this still my pussy?" He hit me with a death stroke. All I could do was nod yes to him.

"Tell me."

"It's yours Kane. I swear it is. Oh my gawd, here I cum again."

"I love you April and we're going to get our shit together. Do you hear me?" He asked going in and out with my legs on his shoulder. He stood up and spread my legs apart and watched himself go in and out.

"I wanna be with you Kane but…" When I said but he went so deep I lost my breath.

"There are no buts. You're still going to be my wife." I didn't say anything because the feeling was so good.

"Are you still going to be my wife?"

"Yes baby. Yes." I came again. He laid back in the bed and asked me to get on top.

"Ride it baby girl. I know you missed it." I rocked back

and forth on him. My head went back as I lifted myself up and down with my hands behind me.

"Oh Fuckkkkk April." He moaned out.

"How much do you love me Kane?" It was my turn to speak.

"A whole lot baby. Shit." He tried to sit up but I stood on my feet and dropped down hard. He fell back and had his hands on my waist. I squeezed my pussy muscles and plopped down.

"Ahhh shittttt. "He sat up real quick and held me tight. His body shook a little as he released his seeds in me. We stayed in the same position for a few minutes.

"I think I just got you pregnant." Both of us laughed because he came hard as hell and in me.

"I'm the only one having your babies' right?"

"Hell yea."

"Then it doesn't matter. Now get up and make love to me in the shower."

"Whatever you want April. The world is yours. You know that." I grinned because Kane always told me that and it's time to start believing him.

The two of us went at it a few more times and if he didn't get me pregnant the first time we had sex; he definitely did one of the other times. Kane refused to pull out and to be honest I didn't make him. After the last round he went downstairs to get some water and his phone went off. Usually I wouldn't check it but I was being nosy.

Tasia: *I can't believe you let them jump me. I thought we had something Kane but I see now I won't ever compare to April. You always said she's the one who got away and well it seems like the two of you found your way back. The way you danced with her I saw love in your eyes, and I can't compete with that. Stay away from me. I don't ever want to hear from you again.* Is what the text read. I started laughing because we really beat the shit out of her.

Kane came back in the room with two water bottles and some Krimpet cakes. I loved those and he would always buy me two boxes when he went to the store.

He handed me one and opened the other one to eat himself. I stared at him as he read the message the girl sent him

146

and all he did was shake his head.

"You good." I asked and opened the top to my water bottle.

"As long as you're here I'm going to always be good." He leaned in to kiss me.

"Get dressed."

"Huh?"

"Put some clothes on." He threw some sweats and a shirt on and I did the same. Yes, my clothes were still here, untouched.

"Where are we going?" I asked him when we pulled up to the airport.

"To Vegas. I want you as my wife before sunrise."

"But Kane we don't have any witnesses."

"They'll have some there." We walked in the airport and he paid for our tickets. The flight left in two hours, so we sat there discussing if I was taking his last name.

Not even twenty-four hours later I was a married woman, and no one could tell me shit except the woman walking in our direction. I felt him squeeze my hand and he told me to stay calm.

"You married her." We were both shocked his mom knew. I only told Essence and he told Stan so one of them must've told her.

"Yup." He said and moved past leaving her standing there stuck on stupid.

"You ok Kane."

"April, I told you before that as long as I have you and our kids I will always be good. We're married, you have my son, you're about to adopt Lexi, and I got you pregnant. There's nothing else I need in my life." Once he said that my heart fluttered. I was deeply in love with this man and prayed we made the right decision. His mom didn't seem happy and I can tell right now she has something up her sleeve. But she better be ready for a fight because now that our family is complete, I'm not going no fucking where.

Stan

"Sean just because you're about to marry my brother doesn't mean you can say what you want to me." I heard Lucy say as I stepped out the shower. She has been staying with us since Stacy kicked her out.

"Lucy you got one more time to come for me and pregnant or not I'm going to tag your ass." I had to throw some clothes on fast and get down there. Sean is no joke with her hands and Lucy has never been a fighter despite all the mouth she has.

"What's going on?" I asked pulling Sean behind me. She was going on six months and Lucy was not about to make her lose my kid.

"Stan your sister is dirty. She acts like I'm her maid and she disrespects me on a regular." I glanced at Lucy who shrugged her shoulders like she could care less about what Sean said. Sean never told me this was going on, so I was a little surprised.

"Look Lucy. You're my sister but this is her house and

you need to respect it. If you can't then you got to go." She stood up mad as hell.

Sean and I purchased this house before we came back to have for when we came to visit but had never moved in until a month or so ago. The purpose of me coming back was to give Kane my empire and find somewhere to settle down. Sean ended up falling in love with the area and became close with Essence and my sister April. I'm sure if we left the two of them, along with Sean would probably curse me out.

"Fuck you Stan. I've been thrown out I better places then this." She grabbed her purse and headed towards the door.

"Get out of here before I get my niece to beat your ass again." Sean said and I chuckled. SJ and Lexi asked Sean could they call her their aunt since she's with their uncle and Sean got so happy, she squeezed them tight as hell. Lexi had to tell her to back up and calm down because they only asked a question. The shit with those kids is quite comical.

The day we saw the video of those two fighting Lucy, I was pissed because Lexi knows better but after my attitude went away, my girl and I couldn't stop laughing.

"She didn't beat my ass."

"Just go Lucy." I'm sure she was embarrassed enough and Sean bringing it up made it funnier.

"You would think the person who knows where her ex is would be more important than some chick you squirted in." I ran over to her and snatched her up by the hair.

"Don't ever disrespect my future wife. Do you understand me?" I twisted her arm back. Say what you want but I don't play those types of games.

"Ok. Ok."

"Now where the fuck is he?"

"I don't know Stan, I swear. I said it to make you mad." She was shaking and tears were coming down her face.

"I'm telling you right now if I find out you know where he's been all this time, I'm going to kill you, which is what I should've done that day at the warehouse. You're only spared because we share the same blood. Don't make me regret it. You know how I get down."

"Stan." She yelled out when I walked back to my door.

151

"Get the fuck off my property." I slammed the door and went upstairs to check on my girl.

Sean was quiet and didn't mess with anyone unless they came for her. In my old occupation she is the only one who caught my attention enough to slow me down with the women, killing and all the other illegal shit I was into. My sister saying that shit had me ready to bring my old ways out.

I opened the door and Sean was lying on her side sniffling.

"What's wrong?" I turned her over and wiped her eyes.

"I'm sorry you had to throw her out. Stan, I don't want to go through what April did over Kane's mom and brother." I know she's talking about them breaking up.

"Baby I'm not worried about that and you shouldn't either. Lucy is who she is and nothing she says or does could ever make me leave you."

"I'm sorry for crying. This baby has me…" I pressed my lips against hers to keep her from speaking and made love to her until her body couldn't take it.

****

Sean and I drove over to Kane's house the next day to congratulate him and my other sister getting married. They hopped a plane to Vegas and did it without telling anyone. We were shocked but happy at the same time. His mom tried everything to keep them from being happy and nothing worked.

I left Sean in the room with April who was explaining what happened at the club and how they ended up saying I do. Kane was in the kitchen cooking some shit that smelled like it was burning.

"What up?" I picked up some French fries that he had on a plate.

"Nothing making my wife something to eat." He turned around with a big ass grin on his face.

"It's about time the two of you got it together."

"I know she wanted a big wedding but I'm tired of her breaking up with me thinking someone else is going to break us up. Her ass is stuck now." We both started laughing.

"What your mom say?" He ran his head on his head as he flipped the burgers over, he was making.

"Man, she showed up at the damn airport when we

came back asking me if I married her. I told her yup and left her standing there."

"What's her deal with not liking April? I know she can't believe April would allow that to happen to Lexi."

"To be honest Stan, I have no idea. In the beginning she loved her, but something changed. Whenever I asked my mom what is was, she would go back to that fuck nigga getting her the second time."

"Damn. But check this out." He put a few extra burgers in the pan for Sean and I.

"I think Lucy knows where the ex is." He raised his eyebrows.

"You know she's been staying with us now that Essence and Stacy are back together."

"Yea."

"Well yesterday her and Sean got into an argument and she was like that's why I know where he is. When I ran down on her ass, she claimed she was lying but I don't believe her. I'm going to have her followed."

"Yo, Lucy is bugging the fuck out. Who knew she

154

would grow up being grimy like that?"

"Man, I sure as hell didn't. But if it's true she knew where they were all this time, I told her I was going to kill her."

"Come on Stan."

"Nah Kane. I spared her once but now she's playing with Lexi's life and what I mean by that is, the nigga is probably watching us and can or will strike at any moment."

"The shit has me wondering who he's hiding with." Kane said and turned back around to finish cooking.

He finished and the girls came down to eat with us. Sean ended up saying she wanted to celebrate them getting married at a party. April was happy to come out and inform every one of her marriage. Kane could care less because he felt like they were already married minus the paper.

We left not too long after we ate because they were going to pick the kids up and tell her mom. She's going to be happy but mad she wasn't there, and I didn't want to be there to hear that.

Demetrius

"Damn Demetrius you definitely have some good ass dick." The chick Sherri said after we finished sexing each other down for the second time tonight.

The two of us have been sleeping together ever since the first night she came in my room. Yea, she did some things with Glenn, but he claimed to be ok with it. He had been working with someone trying to find some bitch named Erica. He was becoming obsessed with this woman.

When I asked Sherri if he ever mentioned that name around her, she said it was her ex best friend and she's most likely dead. Evidently, she did something that made Kane remove her from the earth. She mentioned Glenn did something to her kid and she was Kane's baby mother. It made me think about what April said and how scared she looked when he popped up with me.

Now that I think of it, he held his phone up at the warehouse yelling out he had someone's kid. *Nah, he wouldn't do any shit like that.* I ignored my thoughts and finished talking to her.

"You don't have to tell me what I already know." I lit my blunt and laid back in her bed. I had my own place, but I couldn't take the chance of those niggas finding me; especially since Lucy crazy ass has been stalking the hell out of me. See Sherri kept to herself and didn't nag or bother me. She went out doing her and vice versa.

"Whatever nigga. You know there's a flyer going around for a party Saturday for your ex. She supposedly got married and they're celebrating." I sat up on the bed remembering the last time I saw April. She had called me up after her mom got out of the hospital and asked me to meet her. I wasn't worried about her doing anything because she didn't roll like that.

"You're still sexy as ever, even with the stomach." I hugged her and sat down at the restaurant with her.

"Why would you shoot my mom? If you wanted my attention all you had to do was find me like you did the last time?" She was straight to the point.

"I was bugging April and I'm sorry." I could see her

eyes getting watery.

"I told you not to leave and when you weren't there I got pissed and took it out on her."

"Demetrius why don't you want me to be happy?"

"April, you were my girl first. When I went to jail you were supposed to wait for me." She shook her head and started laughing.

"How could you expect me to wait for you when you were beating my ass and constantly cheating on me? I loved everything about you but the abuse became too much and I was actually happy you went to jail. I figured you would change but I see you're still the same selfish nigga you were before you went in." I reached over the table and grabbed her hands.

"Don't let that nigga you with make you believe you're untouchable. That mouth will get you fucked up." She snatched her hands back.

"We're not together anymore." I gave her a shocked look.

"It has nothing to do with you. We are going in different directions that's all and before you ask yes, he is

going to take care of his kid." I had to look at April because she's no longer the weak bitch I was able to control. That nigga gave her some self-esteem or something.

"Anyway, what's going on with Glenn?" She asked sticking a piece of steak in her mouth. She must've ordered both of our food before I came. She knew I only ate a burger and fries when we went to a place, I was unfamiliar with. Hey, you can never go wrong with that unless they don't cook it well done.

"Not much. I haven't really seen him too much. After I went home the day, I left you at the hospital he was at the house with some chick. I saw him a few times after, but he's been out doing his own thing."

"Oh but he's around?" I was curious as why she's asking about a dude, she didn't want around her and called him names.

"Yea, I'm sure. What are all the questions about?"

"Oh nothing. I didn't realize it was him the day at the house and was wondering what he'd been doing in the area." She spoke in a way that made me feel like she was hiding

160

something.

We sat there eating and talking about old times, well the good ones anyway. She told me we would meet up again, but I wasn't so sure about that.

"Are you going?" Sherri asked bringing me out my thoughts

"Nah, but I know your nosy ass is. Do me a favor though?"

"What?"

"Try and get the nigga Kane to fuck you."

"Nigga you trying to pimp me out?"

"Nah, I want to see how into his wife he really is. All men fall victim to pussy."

"You do know I used to mess with him right?"

"That's why it should be easier." I smirked and watched her put clothes on. Sherri had some good pussy and she could suck dick pretty well. I'm sure if she offered the nigga another chance to hit it, he would.

Sherri

Demetrius and I have been sleeping with one another for a while now and a bitch is definitely addicted to his dick. Don't get me wrong, Glenn had a decent sex game, but he wasn't rocking with Demetrius.

However, Kane's is the best and worth going to the party and try to get a little more. He never could deny my head game so I had to make sure to catch him alone and strip his ass faster than he can catch himself.

Demetrius gave me some money to go shopping. He said if I were playing the part my outfit had to be on point or he wouldn't even look in my direction. At first, I thought he wasn't going but imagine my surprise when I got home from the mall today and he informed me that we would go together. He wanted to see his ex and I wanted to see Kane.

He wore some Gucci outfit with the sneakers to match and I wore a black strapless dress giving Kane more access. We complimented each other and left the house with our own thoughts running through our heads.

We stepped in the club and the shit was packed wall to wall with people. I turned to looked at Demetrius and he told me to hurry up and find a spot in the dark. He didn't need anyone to know he was there. After we made it passed the bar, I found a table that was dark and on the side of the DJ. I'm sure people won't come over here and it's the best spot for him to be incognito.

He and I sat there getting drunk from the drinks we kept ordering. Kane and April stepped in after twelve and a bitch was jealous as hell. Kane had money for two or three lifetimes, and he didn't spare any cost when it came to her.

The bitch had diamonds in her ears, around her neck, on her wrist and she had a dress on, some red bottoms where you could see a diamond anklet and that fucking huge ass rock on her finger couldn't be missed. I glanced at Demetrius and his ass was hating too. Kane had on clothes that were guaranteed to be expensive and he was shining bright like April with diamonds everywhere.

They made their way through the crowd speaking and taking photos with people. I watched how he held her hand and kept her close as if he was worried about someone coming for her.

They went up to the VIP section and that's where you could see the rest of the crew. I tossed the last drink back, fixed my clothes and went to handle my business. Demetrius told me not to mess up because this was the only chance, I would be around him so make it count.

Kane got up, said something to April and walked down the steps. Yup, a bitch watched his every move. He opened the bathroom door and before he could close it, I slipped right in. He sucked his teeth and went to relieve himself in one of the stalls. I heard the lock click and was pissed I didn't get a chance to witness that dick. It's all good though because it would be in my mouth soon enough and hopefully my pussy.

"What do you want Sherri?" He asked unlocking the stall. I sat up on the sink with my legs cocked open waiting for him to respond. He smirked and washed his hands at the other sink.

"I miss you Kane."

"Oh yea. What you miss Sherri?" He had his arms

folded as he stood there watching me.

"I miss that big dick going in and out of me." I felt myself getting ready to cum when he moved closer to me.

"Make that pussy cum for me." He whispered in my ear but didn't touch me. His breath smelled of the liquor he drunk.

"I'm cumming Kane." My body shook as my juices leaked down my pussy. I opened my eyes and Kane licked his lips. Someone started banging on the door so he went to open it. If looks could kill I would be dead. April stood outside the door glancing from me to him and ran out with him going after her. *Mission complete.* I gave myself a birdbath and found my way back to Demetrius.

"Did y'all fuck?" He asked slurring his words.

"Nope. But April walked in the bathroom and I was sitting on the sink half naked. She was maddddd." He nodded his head and told me to come here.

"Suck my dick real quick." I gave him just what he wanted. Hell, there was a tablecloth, and no one could see us anyway. After he came, he sat me on his lap and the two of us fucked the hell out of each other. This was a great night all around for me.

Kane

"You think it worked baby?" April asked when she ran up to VIP.

"You know what your husband working with. Of course it worked."

"What does your dick size have to do with anything?"

"She thought she would get some. You know my man makes the women go crazy."

"Yea ok. Make me cut it the hell off." She rolled her eyes and I pulled her into my chest.

"My man only craves you baby." We engaged in a passionate kiss. I sat her down on my lap and her dress lifted a little and my man got hard as hell. As bad as I wanted her, we would have to wait until later.

I saw my brother coming in my direction and April leaned in my ear and told me to relax. He and I still haven't spoken since the fight. I found out he wanted to apologize to both April and I in the hospital that day, but shit went left.

"Hey April." She stood up and gave him a hug. I pulled

167

her dress down because it lifted a little in the back.

"Don't think because we speak now that you still don't have making up to do."

"I know. Essence already got me doing all types of crazy shit around the house and I have to set the wedding up by myself. She said if it isn't nice, she wouldn't walk down the aisle." April busted out laughing and I couldn't help but do the same. That's what his ass gets for putting her through that.

"Well Kane Jr. is coming for the weekend."

"What? Essence didn't tell me." Stacy hated to be around newborns. He felt like they were too small, and he would hurt them.

"Too bad. The kids will be there to help."

"Oh hell no. I'd rather keep Kane Jr. alone then have those two running around."

"First of all. Don't talk about my daughter and her cousin like that. You know they're misunderstood."

"Mannnn misunderstood my ass." She laughed.

"Be good baby. He's trying." She whispered in my ear and kissed my lips. I nodded my head and watched her walk over to Essence and Sean. I don't know where the hell Stan went.

"Look man. I'm not going to give a long speech, but I do want you to know I'm sorry. I fucked up and couldn't take Essence leaving me. I never meant to disrespect April or make you leave your family unprotected. You know I love my niece and April been around us forever."

"Don't ever do that shit again Stacy or I swear you won't ever hear from me again." He told me he understood and gave me a hug. I did miss us hanging out but he had to respect my family like I did his.

"So you married her huh?"

"Yea man. She owns my heart and I'll be damned if another man slides in to try and take my spot."

"April ain't never leaving your ass." I laughed because he was right. Her ass wasn't going anywhere.

"Are you guys finished making up? Stacy, I wanna dance." Essence said whining. The two of them always stole the show on the dance floor.

"Take your nasty ass down there. I don't know why you

just don't go fuck him in the car. I mean why do we have to watch you dry jump on the floor?" I shook my head laughing at April.

"Ugh ah bitch. Don't come for us when you and Kane do the same thing." April stuck her middle finger up and sat on my lap.

"Yo. Let me rap to y'all real quick." Stan said with a look on his face that made us stand right up.

"Don't leave out of this section."

"Ok."

"I mean it April."

"Essence that means you too." Stacy told her and we followed Stan. We went out a side door and saw two dudes whooping some guys' ass. Whoever he was laid in a fetal position barely moving. The closer we got, the more familiar he looked. I'll be damn if it wasn't my wife's ex. I'm not even going to describe what he looks like because there's no explanation for it.

"What do we have here?" Stacy said kicking him in the stomach.

"Fuck you." He had the nerve to yell out with his mouth dripping with blood.

"It looks like you're the one fucked."

"You're about to get fucked now that your ass was caught in the bathroom with Sherri." He spit more blood out thinking the shit was hilarious.

I had to laugh at him because April and I were both aware Sherri came to the party. However, we didn't know she came with him but that makes it even better. If she fucked with him then most likely she knew where Glenn was. I will deal with her later.

April told me to go to the bathroom and if Sherri follows let her do whatever, but she can't touch me, which was fine with me. Stan was going to wait for April to run out the bathroom and follow Sherri. I guess she led him straight to this bum nigga.

"You fucking with real niggas here. Me and my wife had the shit planned." I could see how shocked he was out of the one eye that wasn't closed.

"Me and my wife are a team and it doesn't require me to put my hands on her either. You fucked up with a real woman and I thank you because had you not, I may have never met my wife and had my son."

"It won't last. Sherri is gonna kill her."

"She can try but you can believe that dumb bitch falls victim to my dick. I will have her in the ground within the next twenty-four hours."

"Where is that fuck nigga Glenn?"

"Looking for your daughter." He laughed hard and I found myself beating the shit out of him and fucking him up worse.

"Get rid of this piece of shit." I told Stan and stood up.

"No. I want to do it." April came walking towards us with Sean and Essence. Her ass does not know how to fucking listen.

"I told your ass to stay inside."

"I know but I was bored and missing you." She walked up and kissed me before turning around and grabbing the gun out of Stan's hand.

"This is for all the abuse I endured when I was with you and for shooting my mother." He didn't say anything but you could tell he felt bad. She shot him a few times in the face and then another in the arm and stomach. I guess she needed to make sure he was dead. She handed the gun back to Stan as Essence and Sean stood there shaking their heads.

"I'm ready to go home and let you fuck the shit out of me." She said and walked away. Watching her ass sway back and forth had my dick hard and me running behind her. April has always been tough but her shooting the gun and telling me she wants to fuck made me look at her in a different light.

****

Over the next few days we had someone watching Sherri's every move hoping to catch her with Glenn, but it never happened. The dude called today and told me she was in a restaurant with my mom and that shit had me thirty-eight hot. She kicked Sherri out the hospital room when my daughter was in there and now, she's having lunch with her. What the fuck am I missing?

I told April we were having a meeting but never told her with whom. If she saw this shit happening in front of me, she would black out on both of them. I walked over to where they sat, pulled a chair up and joined them. The look of shock on their face was evident.

"So. I wasn't invited to this lunch?" I asked grabbing a biscuit off the table.

"What are you doing here?" My mom had the nerve to ask like she wasn't in the wrong.

"The question is what are you doing here and with her? She's not my wife." My mom sucked her teeth and Sherri sat there grinning.

"Don't you think I should have lunch with one of your kids' mother." I didn't even flinch when she said that dumb shit. If it were the case and Sherri is pregnant, it damn sure ain't mine.

"Yup and again, she's not my wife. You know my wife. She's the one who smacked you and has my other kids." I took a bite of my biscuit and smiled. My mom was being very vindictive, and the shit was becoming tiring.

"Oh, by the way. She's pregnant again." My mom and Sherri's mouth hit the floor. If April was pregnant, we didn't know yet because it would've just happened. I knew it would make both of them mad though.

"You're just going to continue sleeping with her without a condom knowing she's a ho." I shook my head because she was putting a show on for Sherri, but I was about to have the last laugh.

"My wife has never been a ho. This one you're having tea parties with, well now she's a different story. You see while you're sitting here kicking April's back in, good ole Sherri here has been fucking with the same man who violated your granddaughter." Now I wasn't sure about that, but Sherri's reaction told me I'm right.

"Is that true Sherri?"

"Yea Sherri is it true?" I asked sipping some water out one of the glasses on the table. I have no idea why restaurants had so many glasses of water on a damn table.

"I didn't know he did that in the beginning and when I found out I left him alone."

"So you knew it was my daughter and never said a word?" She put her head down.

I was getting ready to let both of them have it when my wife walked in with Essence and right then and there, I knew I had fucked up. She came to where we sat and I could see hurt on her face. I tried to speak but she wouldn't allow me to get a word out. I didn't say anything because to be honest I could see how it would look crazy.

"Well I see you finally got the family you wanted." April said to my mom who smirked.

"Actually, Sherri here just informed us about her pregnancy with my son." My mom tossed the napkin on her empty plate and stood up.

"That's great because you'll be able to see at least one of his grandchildren."

"Umm Lexi is my grandchild and she will always be around."

"That's where you're wrong." April gave her a fake smile.

"I signed those adoption papers in court yesterday and she is legally my child. Therefore, I have say so over her whereabouts. And your son here, well, he's not going to accommodate you because he's going to be too scared to go against me or bring his ass home." I didn't say shit because she spoke the truth. There's no way in hell I was taking my ass home tonight. April will not kill me in my sleep and little did my mother know Lexi doesn't want to see her. That's why my pops had been coming to the house all week to spend time with the kids.

"It's sad when a woman as old as you, has so much time on your hand, you meddle in your son's affairs. But you can continue because enough is enough. Kane, you think because we're married, I won't leave you. Think again. I'm over this shit with your mother and ex. Enjoy your life."

"Damn it's about time. I should've had you around a lot sooner had I known it would make you leave."

"Ma, that's enough. Tell me right now why the fuck you don't like her. I'm not playing these fucking games with you any longer." I could see my mom's face and she was ready to smack me but I was over the shit. April and Essence stood there waiting along with me.

"I don't like her because she has AIDS."

"WHAT?" All of us screamed out.

"Kane, I pray you didn't catch it. Your kids need you and if you stay with her it's not going to end well. You have to believe your kids are more important than her."

"First of all, I don't have any diseases. Just so your illiterate ass know they take all those tests when you go in the hospital to give birth. And if I did have, it I would never pass that shit on to anyone." April told her and my mom stood there stuck.

"Who the fuck told you some dumb shit like that?" She looked at Sherri who tried to back away from the table, but April and Essence already started beating on her.

I didn't even step in and I didn't allow anyone else to either. Sherri deserved every bit of the ass whooping they were giving her. Why in the hell would she tell my mom some shit like that anyway? And if I had it why is Sheri hell bent on sleeping with me? This is the shit I be talking about when it comes to dumb bitches getting good dick. They don't know how to fucking act.

"If you guys don't leave, I'm going to call the cops." The manager said standing next to me. I grabbed April and Essence off Sherri and told them to take their ass home. Sherri got up off the floor and limped her ass out the restaurant. I turned around and looked at my mother with disgust.

"Take your ass home and get it together. Tomorrow you're going to bring your ass to my house and apologize to my fucking wife and daughter for all the shit you've been starting."

"Kane, I'm the mother."

"You heard what the fuck I said. Don't do it and you will regret it." I told her and walked out the restaurant trying to figure out how I'm going to handle my wife. I walked out and Sheri had her car headed straight for April. I don't know why they didn't leave like I told them.

"I told your ass to go home." I snatched her out of the road just in time.

"Did that bitch try and run me over?"

"I'm going to handle that. Take your ass home like I said and Essence don't take your ass over there either."

"Nigga you're not my…" I looked at her and she closed her mouth.

"Bye bitch. Your ass in trouble and don't call me on your death bed." Essence walked as fast as she could even with her slight limp.

I parked down the street from Sherri's house and watched her go inside holding her face. I had no remorse for what my wife and Essence did to her. Once she tried to run April over it was time to let her know who she's fucking with. I knocked on her door and the dummy answered. She had to think I was someone else.

"Kane I'm sorry." Were the first words that escaped her mouth. I pushed her back and closed the door. You could tell how scared she was but too bad.

"You tried to kill my girl?"

"Kane what did you expect? Her and Essence jumped me."

"Now I can ask you the same question. What did you

180

expect when you told my mom she had AIDS?"

"I was mad you wouldn't fuck with me."

"How did you end up kicking it with my mom's?" I had to know before I ended her life.

"One day I saw your mom in the store, and I asked her how you were. First, she rolled her eyes and said happy with his woman. That shit pissed me off so I told her April had AIDS and she believed me." I didn't even wait to hear anything else come out her mouth and shot her right between the eyes. What type of woman comes up with a story as reckless as that? I called Stan up and had him send someone to clean this mess up.

April

"I'm sorry Kane. I should've left when you told me to."

I was standing at the door when he came in. He moved past me and went upstairs straight to one of the guest rooms. I started to follow him but then I remembered he's pissed.

I fed the kids and bathed them waiting for him to come help me, but he stayed in that room all night. I took a shower and went to check on him and bring him something to eat. He was in the room smoking and watching television.

"Yo you need to listen when I talk to you." He blew smoke in the air.

"Where you been Kane?"

"Handling business." I sucked my teeth and walked closer to the bed licking my lips.

"Nah April. You were ready to think I would cheat on you and then…" Is all he got out when I crawled on the bed, sat on top and threw my tongue in his mouth. My bottom half moved up and down his shaft over his clothes making him hard.

"Get up April." He managed to get out. He guided my hips on him and I lifted my nightgown shirt over my head. His hands massaged my breasts and I let my head fall back. So much for me getting up.

"You have to show me you deserve this dick after the shit you pulled." He put the blunt out and stared at me.

"I'm sorry baby." I removed his hands from my chest, moved down, and took his basketball shorts and boxers down. My mouth always watered when I came face to face with my best friend.

"How's this baby?" I stopped sucking to ask.

"It's ok." He said smiling and looking down at me. I spit on it and licked down his shaft and went to his balls.

"Damn April. That's exactly why you're my wife." He moaned out as I gave him the business.

"You came a lot." I said and went to slide down but he wouldn't let me.

"Bring that pussy up here." He grabbed my legs and sat me on his face. Kane had me moaning so loud, he told me to cover my mouth with a pillow before I woke the kids. After he let me cum in his mouth a few times he let me down, turned

me over and spread my legs open. Once he entered me, I knew

he would take his frustrations out on me.

"April stop screaming."

"Baby I can't. I'm cumming again and it feels too

good."

"Then I'm gonna pull out." I wrapped my legs around

his back and grabbed his neck to put my tongue in his mouth to

stifle my sounds.

"Fuckkkkk April." He moaned out and we both

released together. He fell on the bed next to me.

"Kane, I'm not sure why she told your mom that but…"

"April, if I even thought you had something my dick

would've never touched you. Don't worry about shit like that

because you know she was being childish, and my mother

should've known the shit too." I could see how much it

stressed him out his mom was doing dumb shit. He and I

showered and went back in our room to go to sleep.

I woke up out my sleep in a cold sweat from having a

nightmare about killing my ex. It was because I took his life but more so how he taunted me in my dream about Glenn coming back for Lexi. I moved the covers off my body and went in the bathroom to relieve myself.

Staring at myself in the mirror had me thinking about all the shit happening. I turned the shower on, slid my clothes off and hopped in. The hot water felt good beating down on my skin. After twenty minutes of being in there and clearing my head I shut the water off and grabbed a towel to dry off.

"Mommy, can you come lay with me." I looked up and Lexi was standing at the door crying.

"What's wrong?" I pulled her in for a hug and she continued crying and squeezed me harder.

"If I tell you something will you promise not to say anything?" She asked me. I shut the bathroom light off, grabbed my robe and walked back in the room with her. I turned the light on and had her sit there for a minute while I went back to my room to throw some clothes on. Kane was staring at me when I opened the door.

"What's up babe?" He yawned and got up to use the bathroom.

"Where you going?" I turned around and he stood there in just his pajama pants looking sexy as hell. I couldn't focus on that right now when my daughter needed me.

"I woke up from a bad dream sweaty and took a shower."

"Stop staring at me April." I smirked and walked over to him on the bed.

"Lexi wants to talk to me but I think you should come too."

"Did she ask for me?" He laid back down.

"No."

"April, she probably wants to talk girl stuff." He threw the pillow over his head.

"Kane get up and come on." I grabbed his hand.

"Yo, I swear if it's nothing I'm fucking you up." He slid his feet in his slippers and followed me to her room.

We opened the door and she was sitting on the bed Indian style watching cartoons. She turned to look at us and ran over to her father and cried again. He lifted her up and walked over to the bed to sit down. Her body was shaking and she kept asking him not to put her down. He looked at me and I shrugged my shoulders. Yes, she cried to me but I still didn't know what was wrong with her either.

After a few minutes he was able to get her to calm down. He had her go in the bathroom to clean her face off. The shit was scaring me because we had no idea why the sudden change but then again, she just woke up so it was probably a nightmare.

"Tell me why you're crying." Kane said and she glanced over at me. I nodded my head for her to say it. She would always look at me if she thought he would yell at her to make sure I stayed in the room.

"Remember a while back when I stayed at Nana's and SJ got in trouble for the video?" We both shook our heads yes and I wanted to laugh when I remembered Essence showing it to me.

"Well nana took me to the store with her and told me to go in the next aisle to get something for her. At first I stared at her because she isn't supposed to let me out of her sight." Kane looked at me and I instantly started getting mad.

Everyone who had Lexi knew since Glenn was nowhere to be found, Lexi had to be watched closely. I mean all kids should be anyway but a child that has gone through what she has should definitely be.

"Some lady she knew started talking to her and so I did what she asked but when I got in the aisle, he was there waiting for me." Kane popped up yelling.

"Who was there Lexi?" She didn't want to answer because her father made her nervous and she started crying.

"Who was there Lexi?" She kept shaking her head no like she didn't want to say.

"The Glenn guy. I don't know how he found us but when I started backing up, he moved closer and grabbed me." Kane paced the room back and forth scaring both of us.

"What did he do Lexi?"

"He tried to make me go in the back with him but I started screaming out stranger danger. At first no one paid me any attention but then the same lady nana had just finished talking to, turned down the aisle and noticed him dragging me by the arm. She called out to nana and she came running. Daddy, I don't know how he keeps finding me, but he does."

"Lexi, I swear on my life I'm going to get him." She nodded her head.

"Mommy, nana said not to tell you because you're going to say its her fault and keep me away from her." I looked up at my husband and he gave me the most hateful stare and stormed out the room. That shit pissed me off and instead of running after him I got in the bed with Lexi and stayed there until both of us fell asleep. I wanted to ask her more questions, but she seemed drained and I didn't want to put too much pressure on her where she would feel like she did anything wrong.

The next morning, somehow, I was in my own bed. I hopped up, ran in Lexi's room and she wasn't in there. For some reason I started panicking and I had no idea why because that motherfucker would never make it pass the gate to get her.

I ran down the steps and found Kane, his mother, SJ and Lexi sitting in the living room. Kane turned to look at me and told me to go back upstairs and get dressed. I wanted to smack the fucking daylights out of his mother as she sat there pretending like what she did was ok.

I made Lexi come upstairs and wait with me. She loved lying in our bed and watching television on the big screen her father had to have in here. I swear the light is so bright at night, I had to use pillows to cover my face to sleep if he's still awake watching it.

I came out the bathroom, grabbed something to throw on and went back in there to get dressed. I brushed my teeth and washed my face but at the same time told myself to remain calm. Kane came in the bathroom as I washed my face and wrapped his arms around my waist from behind. He placed kisses down my neck and sucked on it gently. I tried to push him back because it was turning me on and his mom's downstairs and Lexi's in the room.

"Do you need me to relieve some stress before you go down there?"

"No because..." I didn't even finish, and he had my pants and panties down to my ankles forcing his way in and I loved every minute of it.

"Throw it back April." He moaned in my ear and played with my clit.

"Kane, I love you so much baby." That didn't do anything but make him go harder. I felt him going a little low so he could dig deeper. He had to cover my mouth because he knew screams were about to come out.

"I love you too and don't you forget that. Damn, this pussy is always wet and tight for me." He moved a little faster.

"Get me pregnant Kane." He grabbed the back of my hair and pumped even faster. I threw my ass back on him and he couldn't stop himself from cumming. A few minutes later he hopped in the shower with me. We both wanted to go another round but decided against it since we were already in there for a while.

When we came out the bathroom his mother stood in our room shaking her head. Luckily, we got dressed in there otherwise she would've seen us naked. Kane started massaging my shoulders trying to keep me from going off.

"That couldn't wait?" She had the nerve to say.

"You couldn't keep your ass downstairs?" I responded not giving two fucks how she felt about my comment.

We all stepped out the room and you could hear SJ and Lexi down stairs arguing about something. When I got in the room they looked up and SJ dropped the iPad on the floor. His dad brought him a new one after he broke the other one from being angry. Kane picked it up and laughed.

It was a game and evidently Lexi was whooping his ass in it. Kane asked why they were arguing, and Lexi said because he wanted to keep restarting it.

"Do you want to explain why in the hell you left my child unattended in the store to run your mouth? Or how that nigga got close and almost got her again?" Her eyes got wide as hell and she glanced over at Lexi who covered her face in Kane's chest as she sat on his lap.

"Why did you do that nana?" SJ asked and stood up. Kane gave him a look that made him sit his ass back down. SJ hated anyone to hurt Lexi or any of the women in the family. The one thing I could say is if no one could handle him, Kane sure could.

"First of all…" She said but I cut her off.

"First of all nothing. How dare you tell my child not to tell me or even her father for that matter?" She didn't say anything.

"My mother taught me never to disrespect my elders but it went out the window the second you accused me of allowing a man to harm her. Now I'm going to ask you again. Why would you tell her not to tell us? Is it because you couldn't figure out how to tell him you fucked up? Or because you thought I would rub it in your face that things happen beyond our control and we can't help it?

"Kane."

"Don't call him. He can't help you this time." I told her and he sat there not saying a word. That's why my husband is the shit. He knew his mom was dead ass wrong and let me handle her accordingly. This time I wouldn't lay hands on her unless it warranted it.

"I came over here to apologize for being a bitch because of what Sherri told me; not to be interrogated about something that happened weeks ago." I shook my head

193

laughing. This woman refused to admit how wrong she is and tried to bypass the entire conversation.

"I don't need an apology for that and had we known weeks ago it would've been addressed then. Don't you sit here making what you did less of an issue than it is. My child is having nightmares again and it's partly your fault. Had you called someone that day he may have been caught but you were so busy trying to keep it from me, he's lost in the wind again."

"I don't have to listen to this shit." She grabbed her things and stood to leave.

"SIT YOUR ASS DOWN AND LISTEN TO EVERYTHING SHE HAS TO SAY." I heard a voice coming from behind me say. Kane's dad had Junior in his hands with Stacy and Essence walking in behind him. They kept him overnight and his dad must've driven over here with them.

"I'm a grown woman who."

"A grown woman who has caused more than a little bit of problems with this family. I'm telling you right now if you don't make shit right our lawyer will be called to file for a separation. This has gotten way out of hand and everyone is tired of it.

"SJ and Lexi go upstairs." Stacy and Kane both said at the same time. The two of them ran out the room. Kane's dad handed him the baby and told everyone to sit.

"What you did is unacceptable, and you should be sitting here apologizing for all of it and not certain things. April is her mother regardless of what you think." His mom rolled her eyes.

"She may not have birthed her but she may as well have. April has never mistreated her and she was devastated over what happened to Lexi and instead of you being the mother in law who used to love her, you turned and started blaming her. Then something similar happens while Lexi was in your care, but everyone is supposed to look the other way because it's you." His mom had tears coming down her face but that shit didn't faze me at all. People can say that's messed up I feel this way but after everything she put me through she deserves to cry.

"Kane, I'm sorry for allowing that man to even attempt to take her." Kane shook his head in disbelief and so did everyone else. This woman refused to acknowledge me being her mother, stepmother, or any type of female figure in her life at all.

"It's ok baby."

"No it's not April. Ma, if you can't respect my wife and the fact she is Lexi's mother then you and I won't ever have a relationship. Other people may allow their moms to disrespect their women but I'm not. I think it's time for you to go." He lifted me off his lap and helped her up out the chair. No one said a word and you could tell she was hurting but fuck it.

I knew this would hurt him because he loved his mother, but I can't make him do what he doesn't want. I've left him alone, stayed away for a while hoping it would help him and his mom become close again but he's dead set on not dealing with her if she can't deal with me.

"Kane please listen to me."

"Are you going to respect my wife?" She didn't say anything.

"Then there's nothing for me to listen to." He opened the door and she stepped out on the porch wiping her eyes.

"I can't believe you are choosing…"

"Stop right there ma." He told her and we all sat there listening to him try and remain calm.

"Before you even think about blaming her know this. You're about to accuse her of something she told me not to do."

"What are you talking about?"

"She told me not to stop speaking to you and make sure you get to know your grandson. You are so busy trying to hurt her and she forgave your childish ass a long time ago. No, she may not speak to you but she has sat back time and time again letting you treat her like shit. That day in the hospital she was at her breaking point and not because you came for her but because you came for Lexi. You know my daughter, she has legally adopted and taken care of before knowing who I was." She sucked her teeth.

"I think it's better for you to stay away from my family until you can come to grips that she's going to be in my life forever. She's going to have all my babies and I better not ever hear you bring up to any of my kids that Lexi isn't hers or what happened to her in the past. Do I make myself clear?"

"Crystal clear but hear this." She stepped in and looked at me.

"I'm happy, that you're happy but I don't have to like her. She may be your wife, but she isn't anything to me and if you think I'm going to kiss her ass to see my grandkids you are sadly mistaken."

"That's your loss. My kids won't miss what they don't know." He told her and shut the door in his face. None of us spoke a word after that. Kane went to the bedroom and I stayed in the living room talking to everyone else. His mom is a piece of work and honestly, he can say he's ok with the outcome but I wasn't.

After everyone left, I started making dinner because we were having Lasagna and it takes a while to make. I also made a fresh salad with garlic bread to go along with it.

Kane must've smelled the food because he brought his ass downstairs with all the kids. Lexi came in asking to help

198

and I had her take the lettuce out and rinse it under the water. She did what I asked while Kane and SJ sat at the table playing some card game. The family may be a little dysfunctional, but we were still one in the same when it came to spending time with the kids.

Essence

"What you think April?" I asked opening the curtain as I came out the dressing room. I had her with me trying on wedding dresses today.

After the week we had between our mother in law and the guys trying to find this pervert we needed a break from the madness. We each hired a nanny and it's the best thing we could have ever done. There's no more running to grandmas all the time. It wasn't that I had a problem with my mother in law but April's my best friend and has been way before Kane or Stacy came in our lives. I tried not to take sides, but their mom is dead ass wrong for how she's treating April.

"I don't know about this one Essence." I looked down at it and laughed. It had mad ruffles on the sleeves and around the waist area. It reminded me of a dress the women wore back in the olden days and I'm not sure why I even tried it on.

"It does look crazy." She went over to the rack and found a few more dresses for me to try on.

After two hours of searching, I finally found one that looked beautiful on me. I paid the woman for it and she ordered a new one while we stood there. I may like this one but I'm sure other women tried it on and I refused to wear it. The lady told me it should be in, in three to four weeks. The alterations can be done at that time just in case my weight went up or down. I could've snapped on her but she's right being I was pregnant again. I hadn't told Stacy yet, or even April for that matter. I took a test a few days ago and planned on mentioning it but then all the drama took place, so I left it alone.

April and I decided to stop by this food place called The Avenue that sold different types of food; from Italian to West Indian and Soul food. It's weird to see it all on one menu but hey if it works then I say do it.

The waitress sat us down and took our order. I noticed April being a little standoffish when we got there and waited for her to put the phone down to ask her. She had been texting Kane and checking up on Lexi who had another nightmare last night. I don't care what anyone says, Lexi is her child. Fuck whose stomach she came out of. Their bond was special, and no one could break it no matter how hard they tried.

"What's up April?" I asked when she placed the phone on the table.

"Kane wants another baby and, in the beginning, so did I but now he and his mom are on the outs. I'm not sure if it's a good time to bring another baby in the world."

"Bitch are you pregnant?" I asked.

"Probably. We never use protection and I don't make him pull out. I mean, come on Essence. How would it sound me telling him we can't have any kids because of his mom?"

"You would sound crazy and he would probably be pissed off." I stared at her and could see the entire situation bothered her.

"April, you can't allow his mom to have control over the decisions you make with your husband. Hence; your husband. If you did, you're never going to be happy." I told her and she nodded like she understood but did she.

April wasn't the type of woman to let anyone get in her head but his mom is definitely causing too many problems then she cares to admit. She and I finished eating and our conversation barely existed, and the shit now bothered me.

When we finished I dropped her off at home and made my way over to my mother in law's house. Stacy and I would be married soon enough but I still called her that. She was sitting on the front porch looking pitiful, but she brought it on herself. She prided herself on being around the grandkids, so I know it was killing her they weren't around like they used to be. I walked up on the porch and she had some wine in a glass sipping on it.

"Hey sweetie." I have no idea why she adored me and hated April but I'm about to find out.

"Hey." I gave her a hug and sat down next to her.

"How's my bad ass grandson?" She laughed and took another sip.

"He's fine and so are your other grandkids." She sucked her teeth.

"Listen. I'm not sure why you have all this animosity towards April but if you don't stop your grandkids will grow up without knowing you and you can forget about Kane."

"Kane will come around. He always does." I chuckled when she said it. Her ass is in complete denial that Kane refuses to fuck with her.

"Why don't you like April? I mean you were all for their relationship before the nonsense Sherri told you. And even after you found out it was a lie you still refuse to be cordial."

"She's going to be just like Erica. That's why I don't like her."

"What are you talking about? She's nothing like that woman and I think you know it." She tossed her head back laughing.

"That's the problem with everyone thinking she will be different. You see Erica and Kane's relationship started out the exact same way. He loved everything about that woman and worshipped the ground she walked on. My son gave her everything she wanted and there isn't anything anyone could tell him bad about her." She said still taking sips. I think her ass was feeling the effects of the wine because she almost fell off the chair when she tried to stand up.

"The minute Kane got locked up everything he had with her went down the drain. The engagement, the love she had for him an even the baby she became pregnant with." I covered my mouth because I was unaware Erica became pregnant by Kane prior to him getting arrested.

"Yup. The bitch called me up and said she couldn't handle having another baby with him being in jail and said she was getting rid of it. I never told Kane because he was locked up and would've probably bugged out and gotten more time. The bitch was selfish and the day she dropped her off to you and my son, is the best decision she's ever made in her life." She was telling me things I didn't know but she still had no reason to dislike April.

"Kane was hurt over that and I'll be damned if I allow my son to go through it again. Essence you have a son and one on the way, so you'll see what I'm talking about in a few years when SJ starts dating."

"Who told you I was pregnant?"

"Girl, your hips are spreading and so is your nose. If Stacy doesn't know its because he's not paying attention." She laughed and I did too.

"April is nothing like Erica and if you haven't noticed she will go through hell and high water to protect Lexi. I know you blame her for that man getting her but she went through some things herself when it happened. She even broke up with Kane over it because she called herself a failure for entertaining Erica that day in the mall. No matter how much Kane told her he didn't blame her, she blames herself but you doing it too makes it harder for her to forgive herself. I'm not sure why you think she would hurt Kane or Lexi because she's not like that. I'm not just saying that since she's my friend. I'm saying it because it's the truth."

"I don't know Essence. She disrespected me and…" I put my hand up and stopped her right there.

"You brought it on yourself. She tried to keep her composure, but you continued pushing her until she couldn't take anymore. You have to take responsibility for your part in all this too."

"I'm not sure Kane will ever forgive me now." I saw the tears falling down her face.

"You are his mother and yes you two aren't speaking but he forgives you. What he won't forgive is how you're treating his wife who has done nothing to you. Do you think he likes not speaking to you? He wants you around all his kids but at the same time she is his wife and you have to respect her." She didn't say anything and nodded her head.

"Let me get out of here. Stacy is looking for me and SJ has to be picked up from one of his friends' house. I'll speak to you later." She gave me a hug and I left. That woman is going to have to deal with her own demons before she can deal with anyone else. Her beef with Erica trickled down to April and that's fucked up.

I picked SJ up and pulled up at my house and saw a car there I've never seen before. We got out and my son ran to the door to open it but the door was locked. I used my keys to open it and almost lost my mind when I witnessed Lucy's crazy ass naked on my fucking couch. I screamed for SJ to go upstairs and find his dad. I swear if the nigga was coming out the shower or even looked guilty that he slept with this bitch in my house I was killing both of them. I dropped my things and made my way to where she was and stood in front of her smirking.

"I see your crippled ass made it home just as we finished. Damn, I missed Stacy's dick." She had the nerve to say and all I saw was red and started beating the shit out of her. I could hear my son screaming and I wanted to stop but my adrenaline was pumping so bad I couldn't.

Somehow the bitch got on top of me and I felt her scratching my face. I flipped her over and grabbed the African Statue sitting on the living room table and hit her over and over with it. Blood squirted on my face and it wasn't until someone picked me up off her.

I looked and her face was mangled and it looked like her arm was dislocated. Stan bent down to check her pulse and shook his head. I started crying because I've never killed anyone and to do it in front of my son made me feel like shit.

Stacy came running in afterwards and told me he didn't even know she was in the house. He didn't ask any questions, carried me upstairs, stripped me down and put me in the shower. He put soap on a rag and washed me up.

"Is mommy ok?" I heard SJ asking from the door.

"She's fine son. Go in your room and don't come out until I tell you." I could hear him run off.

"Am I going to jail?" I asked him and he didn't say anything at first.

"Stop crying Essence and don't ask me any dumb shit like that. You know I would never allow anything to happen to you." He wrapped a towel around me and helped me dry off and put some pajamas on.

"I'll be back."

"Stacy can you send SJ in here?" He told me yes and a few minutes later my son came crawling in the bed with me. He wiped my eyes and told me to stop crying.

"Ma, she had it coming to her." I looked at him and he had the remote in his hand changing the channels.

"SJ don't say that. No one deserves to die."

"That's what uncle Stan said to Kane over the phone." It means April knew what happened and I'm sure she'd be calling or coming over.

"Oh yea."

"Yea. He said something about her being with the guy that did bad things to Lexi and they were looking for her." I covered my mouth.

Lucy is a grimy bitch and she should've told Stan where that man was. I'm sure she knew what he did and even if she didn't, she knew the guys were looking for him and Demetrius because Stacy said she asked why Kane wanted him dead.

"How are you fighting with my daughter in your stomach?" Stacy said staring n my face when I opened my eyes. I must've fallen asleep lying there with SJ. I asked him what time it was and he told me after two in the morning.

"Who told you I was pregnant?"

"Baby, I know your body better than you. I've known for a while and was just waiting for you to mention it."

"I'm sorry. I found out the other day and I planned on telling you but then that stuff happened with your mom at Kane and April's house and I forgot. I walked in, saw her naked and she said some shit like the two of you had just finished having sex."

"You know I would never."

"I know Stacy. She had that ass whooping coming but I didn't mean to kill her. How did she get in the house? Wait, is Stan mad at me?"

"You must've left the living room window opened because on the camera that's how she got in and Stan isn't mad at all. He's actually happy someone else did it. He's done a lot in his past but it's would've been hard to take his own flesh and blood out. That's like him having to kill April."

"I understand. Stacy can you make love to me?" I asked him and he shut the television off and handled my body so well he put me right back to sleep.

Kane

"What do you want?" I asked my mother when she stopped by the house. April and the kids went over Stacy and Essence house to check on her after the shit with Lucy. I told her Stacy said she was ok but she had to see for herself.

I was on my way out to handle some shit when she knocked so I was aggravated she wanted to speak to me. She is my mom, so I'll give her the time for a few minutes but that's all she's getting.

"Kane, I want to say I'm sorry about everything. I assumed April would do you like Erica and…"

"Why in the hell would you think that? They are nothing alike and that's why I married April."

"I know it now Kane."

"Now?" I asked as if she couldn't tell before.

"When Erica hurt you I wanted to beat her ass myself but your dad told me to stay out of it because you would end up being made at me. So I sat back and did nothing. I did like April don't get me wrong but when the stuff happened with

Glenn, I felt like she didn't handle the situation well an then I ended up in a similar predicament and saw first-hand how things could escalate quickly. Thank goodness there were men in the store otherwise he may have run away with her." I ran my hand down my face because all this time she hated my wife for absolutely nothing.

"I'm not gonna tell you what my wife went through when it happened but not even for a split second did I think she handled it wrong. She did what she could, and I thank God every day for the woman who screamed out and let April find her. Then you made her feel worse that day in the hospital. You did a lot of hateful and deceitful shit to her and I'm telling you now she may have forgiven you but she won't ever fuck with you." I know it sounded harsh, but I'm not sugar coating anything for her when she didn't care how she treated April.

"Can't you make her speak to me?" I chuckled when she asked me that dumb shit. She most likely could care less about speaking to my wife but I know for a fact she missed Lexi and still has yet to meet my son. The day my dad walked in with him I made her leave right away.

"Ma, I would never ask my wife to fuck with someone who treated her as bad as you did. If she wants you to see her kids, then I'll bring them to you, and I wish you would say something about Lexi not being hers.

"I wasn't. I was wrong for saying those things to her knowing Lexi has been calling her mom for a long time. I thought it would push her away but despite everything I did, she stayed by your side and I admire that. Most women would've left already."

"That's because she loves me and nothing you or anyone else can say will make her leave me. I'm good to her and she is the same in return. Ma, April is everything I've ever looked for in a woman and she's good to my kids. No one and I mean no one will ever take her place." She nodded her head and stood up to leave.

"Look. I'll talk to her about allowing you to see the kids but if she says no you have to respect that."

"Kane, those are your kids too."

"You're right but once I found out you were saying those things to Lexi, I agreed the best thing is to keep you far

214

away as possible from them. I wouldn't allow anyone to speak bad about my kid's mother and I damn sure ain't about to let my own mother do it. My kids may grow up thinking its ok to do it since you did and I can't have that. You allowed Lexi to get away with a lot of shit and now that her mother has control, we won't allow her to be like that anymore."

"I understand and I hope she lets me see the kids. I'm sorry Kane." She kissed my cheek and walked to her car. I watched her leave, hit Stan up and told him I was on the way.

The entire drive over all I could think of was how the situation would take place and if I should've brought my wife. I parked behind Stan and Stacy's car and blew my breath out before I walked in. This is a moment that has been a long time coming.

I opened the door and there he was sitting there looking as if he were barely breathing. I stood in front of him and stared. This man in front of me violated my daughter in more ways than one and it was time to get rid of him for my daughter to have peace of mind and also for him not doing this to another kid.

"You were a hard man to find." I told him and poured gasoline on his legs.

"Fuck you."

"Why are those the words men yell out right before they're about to die?" I turned to Stan and Stacy who shrugged their shoulders.

"You violated my daughter and I'm sure other kids. It will give me great pleasure to be the one to take your life." I lit the match and set his legs on fire. He screamed out as I watched him burn. After a minute or two I used the fire extinguisher to put it out. I wasn't done with him yet. I could've beaten his ass, but my brothers handled that already.

When Stan told me they found him this morning watching some kids at a playground, I was sick to my stomach. This man had a serious problem and I couldn't be happier we found him before he inflicted pain on someone else's child.

He told me at first they were just going to watch him until he approached a kid and tried to walk off. Him and Stacy jumped out the car and beat his ass at the park and then put him in the car.

Now here we are watching him scream out in pain as the flesh melted on his legs. I poured gasoline on his stomach and groin area and lit another match. People may think the fire would spread on his entire body but that wasn't the case. I made sure to only cover the areas I wanted burned at the time and if it did move up, I'd put the fire out. I wanted him to suffer as much as possible before he took his last breath.

"You may have gotten away with this before you got here but you fucked with the wrong nigga's daughter. The only reason it took us a minute to find you is because we didn't know what you looked like."

"Just kill me please. I can't take the pain." I laughed at his dumb ass.

"My daughter and all the other kids you did this too couldn't take the pain either, but you didn't care just like I don't." I stayed in there for an hour torturing him until he passed out. I felt like he wasn't feeling anymore pain and took him out of his misery.

After I finished, Stan had people come to clean him up and I took my ass home. It was getting late and my wife called me a few times.

"Why do you smell like fire and gas?" Lexi asked when I walked through the door.

"Lexi you know better than to question your father." April came walking in the foyer area.

"Go upstairs and check on your brother Lexi." She told her and stared at me without saying anything.

"I'll wait for you to shower and burn those clothes before I ask you what happened." I nodded my head and went upstairs.

April knew when to give me my space and right now it was the best thing. I had to think of a way to tell Lexi he wouldn't bother her anymore without telling her I killed him. She can guess all she wants but I never let her know that part of my life.

"Come here Lexi." I yelled out for her once my shower was done and finished my dinner.

"Yea daddy." I sat her on my lap and April started feeding Jr.

"I wanna tell you that we found the guy and he will no longer bother you."

"I know daddy. SJ called me and said he heard his dad telling aunty Essence you handled the guy who hurt me." These kids were nosy as hell and SJ had no business listening to their conversation.

"Thank you daddy." She hugged me tight and stood up.

"Mommy make sure you keep daddy happy during adult time." April wanted to say something but all we both could do was laugh.

After my son ate and she put him to bed, trust me when I tell you she made her husband very happy during adult time and I did the same. It wasn't until we finished when she told me we were having another baby and a nigga couldn't have been happier.

****

Over the next few months, Sean and Stan had a daughter they named Miracle. They call her that because they've been through so much and thought they would lose her. Lexi wanted to stay over there more because the baby was a girl. Stan didn't mind and Sean adored Lexi and that's probably because she dealt with the same thing as a kid. I'm not sure what makes a man have those type of attractions to a child but all child molesters and rapist should be put to death without trial. Why should they breathe another day when they violated someone like that?

Essence and Stacy finally got married and he ended up hiring an event planner. He told her there was no way in hell he could set up a wedding in that short amount of time without help. They were having another baby too and moved out the house. Essence didn't wanna walk around the house Lucy caused so many problems and died in. Stacy gave Essence whatever she wanted thinking he still had to make it up to her for the mess with Lucy. I told him he made up, but he said it wasn't enough.

Last but not least, April still didn't fuck with my mom and neither did Lexi. I did introduce my son to her but she wasn't allowed at my house. People may say I'm fucked up but when you're in a relationship, that person becomes your family as well. When someone treats them the way my mom did April, I have to look at it for what it is.

If my wife doesn't wanna fuck with her I would never force it on her. April told Lexi she eventually had to go over there and she agreed. That is still her grandmother and she should forgive her. Lexi didn't question my wife when she told her to do something. She may have not liked what she made her do but it was done without popping off at the mouth like she did with everyone else.

CPSIA information can be obtained
at www.ICGtesting.com
Printed in the USA
LVHW111616260220
648289LV00003B/380

9 781090 397713